"Please

"Do you have to make a conquest of every woman you meet?" JoNell asked with angry tears.

Jorge Del Toro gazed down at her with smoldering eyes. "Why must you think of it as a 'conquest?' I am trying to tell you how much I find myself wanting you."

Fire was raging now in his slashing green eyes. He took a step closer to her. Suddenly she realized how alone they were on this deserted stretch of beach.

He pulled her to him. "It won't do you any good to scream," he whispered huskily in her ear. "There is not another living soul within a hundred kilometers."

PATTI BECKMAN
has combined her interest in flying and writing to produce *Captive Heart*. She soloed a plane at age sixteen and later flew in the Powder Puff Derby. Ms. Beckman is married to a fellow writer.

Dear Reader:

Silhouette Romances is an exciting new publishing venture. We will be presenting the very finest writers of contemporary romantic fiction as well as outstanding new talent in this field. It is our hope that our stories, our heroes and our heroines will give you, the reader, all you want from romantic fiction.

Also, *you* play an important part in our future plans for Silhouette Romances. We welcome any suggestions or comments on our books and I invite you to write to us at the address below.

So, enjoy this book and all the wonderful romances from Silhouette. They're for *you!*

P. J. Fennell
President and Publisher
Silhouette Books
P.O. Box 769
New York, N.Y. 10019

PATTI BECKMAN
Captive Heart

Silhouette *Romance*
Published by Silhouette Books New York

To my husband Charles
who is the model for all my heroes

SILHOUETTE BOOKS, a Simon & Schuster Division of
GULF & WESTERN CORPORATION
1230 Avenue of the Americas, New York, N.Y. 10020

ISBN: 0-671-57008-0

First Silhouette printing May, 1980

10 9 8 7 6 5 4 3 2 1

Chapter 1

JoNell Carpenter impatiently tossed a long, blond braid back over each shoulder. Her fidgeting fingers drummed the stick of the Cessna 180. She was approaching her destination—Lima, Peru—and becoming more nervous by the minute.

Tension from the long hours at the controls was making her slender body ache. Her eyes felt gritty, her muscles cramped. More than that, however, her inner turmoil was grinding at her nerves. She tried a few long, deep breaths, but they didn't help.

Unexpectedly, the mist cleared briefly. JoNell gasped. In spite of herself, she felt a pleasant tingle as she saw the Peruvian coastline come into view. The blue waters of the Pacific sparkled with a vitality that brought tears to her eyes.

She dabbed away the moisture from her eyes with a tissue that had been wadded up in the right breast pocket of her powder blue jump suit. "It's just beautiful!" she gasped softly, not wanting to waken her tired Uncle Edgar who snored intermittently in the seat beside her.

The magnificent sight of a foreign coastline laid out in all its raw splendor under the wings of the little airplane caught JoNell off guard and made her forget briefly how much she truly disliked what she was doing.

Under other circumstances she would have thoroughly enjoyed the flight down here from the United States. The scenery had been awesome. She had flown over vast panoramas of deep green jungle alternating with patches of brown and yellow deserts. At times she had cleared mountain passes at 13,000 feet with soaring peaks on either side dissolving into the mist. And once she had caught sight of the great Amazon like a silvery python writhing its way through the jungle.

Yes, the countryside was beautiful—but her mission definitely was not. Had it not been for her father resting at home, recovering from a heart attack, she certainly would never have agreed to ferry this airplane to Peru for the notorious Jorge Del Toro.

JoNell knew all about the philandering, South American playboy. Stories about him filled the Spanish language magazines read by the Cubans back home in Florida. JoNell read the Spanish magazines to keep up her fluency in the language. Long ago, she'd grown tired of reading about Del Toro's romantic escapades. Men like Del Toro were ruthless with women. Once they conquered a woman, they grew bored with her and tossed her aside in search of new game.

Del Toro's most recent encounter had involved a beautiful American actress who had a leading part in a movie being filmed in Peru. The actress had dubbed Del Toro "Latin America's Most Ruthless Heartbreaker." Well, a scoundrel like that certainly couldn't break JoNell's heart . . . but of course he wouldn't try. Men like Del Toro moved in the rarified atmosphere of the South American social jet set. His acquaintances ruled the political and economic tides of Latin America. He came from a rich and prominent family. He would hardly notice a small town girl like JoNell!

JoNell nudged Uncle Edgar awake. The two of them flew in awed silence as they admired the breathtaking view of the Peruvian coastline. The radio hissed and crackled when JoNell called the Lima tower for permission to land. Over the static, she heard a male voice give the wind direction and velocity. She picked her runway, brought the plane down in a smooth, skillful landing and taxied glumly to the hangar.

"That's it," sighed JoNell. She turned off the ignition

and watched the spinning arc of the prop come to a halt. "We're actually here."

"Now that wasn't so bad, was it?" drawled Uncle Edgar in his slow, deep voice. He faced her squarely. His lips curved ever so slightly to indicate that he was smiling.

"Oh, Uncle Edgar," she exclaimed impatiently, "can't you ever really smile like ordinary people do?"

JoNell was immediately ashamed of herself as she saw the blood drain from Uncle Edgar's long, homely face as his hint of a smile turned into a hurt frown.

"I'm sorry, Uncle Edgar," she apologized swiftly, touching his big hand. "I truly am. It's just that I'm so uptight, I'm looking for an excuse to pick on somebody."

She hoped he believed her, because she honestly was sorry. Uncle Edgar was the last person she would ever want to hurt. He had seen her through mumps, chicken pox and the flu. She had trailed around after him ever since she'd been big enough to carry a wrench. In his slow, plodding way, he had talked to her about engines and airplanes for hours on end. He had taught her to love and understand machinery.

Now she had verbally attacked him for a facial mannerism she had come to love. What was wrong with her?

"I know, Pet," he drawled slowly. "I understand. You don't really want to be here, do you? But you feel you don't have any choice. So you're just looking to take your anger out on somebody, and I guess I'm the handiest target. Sure, I understand. Don't worry your pretty head about it."

"Okay, Uncle Edgar," she choked, "you're the most—the most—"

"I know," he said, and patted her hand clumsily.

JoNell looked at her Uncle Edgar through a mist of

tears. He had to be the most compassionate and forgiving man in the world. But then, why not? He'd been through some miserable times with his alcoholism. He'd sunk pretty low. When he finally joined Alcoholics Anonymous and went on the wagon, he spent a lot of time repenting the trouble he'd caused everyone. So he could certainly understand how it is possible to lash out at someone you love when you're not feeling like yourself. And JoNell Carpenter definitely wasn't feeling like herself right now.

"I wonder what he's really like?" JoNell mused, her thoughts again turning to the buyer of the plane she was delivering, the notorious Jorge Del Toro. She raised the door handle, swung around and climbed down. Her sneakers touched Peruvian soil, but right now she wished herself back home in good old south Florida, where the sun was hot and bright every day and the palm trees whispered their secrets to the blue sky. Instead, here she was in damp, chilly Lima, Peru, south of the equator, on a mission she didn't want but couldn't refuse.

"All Peruvian men are dashing, charming, good-looking, suave—terrific lovers and terrible husbands," drawled Uncle Edgar, with a hint of a twinkle in his eyes.

"Oh, Uncle Edgar," she giggled, "now you've done it. You've ruined my beautiful gloomy mood!" And she broke into a merry laugh, her large, brown eyes coming to life for the first time since they had landed the red and white Cessna.

"It's about time," said Uncle Edgar. "Now, let's find this joker and get this transaction completed."

JoNell was all in favor of getting this business over with as quickly as possible. But she faced the irksome prospect of being stuck here in a foreign country, far from home, while she gave flying lessons to a rich playboy. She felt like someone who had been dreadfully miscast in a play. She was a small town girl whose only ambition in life was to be a good teacher in an elementary school. The only kind of man she was interested in meeting was a steady, decent type who'd want to marry her and live a simple, uncomplicated life with her while they raised a small family. Galavanting off to South America had not been part of her plans.

JoNell and her uncle began walking toward the hangar. A fine mist settled around them, making JoNell shiver. She had read that the *garua,* as the mist is called, occurs during the Peruvian winter months from May to October. Mingling with a fog, it obscured the surrounding mountains. Above, the gray sky looked neither threatening nor inviting, just impersonal. JoNell had also read that it never froze in Lima, but she hadn't expected the damp chill to penetrate so deeply.

A heavy, short, dark-haired man materialized wraith-like out of the mist. *"Bienvenidos,"* he said cheerfully, bowing politely to JoNell and offering his hand in welcome to Uncle Edgar.

"Sorry, I don't speak Spanish," Uncle Edgar apologized. "But my niece here speaks your language fluently."

"That good, señor." He rattled off a polite greeting to JoNell in rapid-fire Spanish, flashing a white-toothed smile, but then returned to thickly accented English. "For you, señor, I speak the English, which I do with much good. You Americans, no?"

"Yes," replied JoNell a bit impatiently. "May we go inside? It's awfully cold out here in the rain."

"Rain, señorita? But it never rains in Peru," he chuckled. "This is only a little mist. Come. I take you to dry place. You be more *comodo.*"

"Thanks," JoNell answered gratefully.

"De nada," said the man as he led them through the hangar door, past airplanes of all sizes and colors, and into a small, well-lighted office.

9

"First, we check you through customs," said the man. "Then. . . ."

"Customs?" JoNell asked with surprise. "But don't we have to go through customs in the main terminal with everybody else?"

"Oh, but you see, señor Del Toro instruct customs officer to come here. More—con—con—easy," said the man with a broad smile. "Please, be sit. Everything taken care of for you."

JoNell and her uncle sat on a small green vinyl sofa near the door where they had entered. "Looks like money talks," JoNell said under her breath.

"You're right," Uncle Edgar murmured. "It got you here."

"And how. I certainly wouldn't be here for any other reason!"

JoNell settled back against the sofa and glanced around the room. To her right was the door they had entered. To her left was a worn and battered wooden desk with a bare top. Behind it stood a metal file cabinet. The wall was covered with sectional maps used in airplane navigation. There were two uncomfortable looking straight-back chairs and another sofa, a twin of the one she was sitting on.

With a sudden homesick pang, JoNell envisioned the little airport office her parents owned back home. She sorely wished she were back there now, taking phone calls, filling in the Link trainer when her parents were busy, giving a few flying lessons.

"Uncle Edgar, do you think I did the right thing?" she asked suddenly. "I mean, do you think I did right by insisting on coming here?"

He gave her a long, slow look. She had long ago given up any hope of prodding Uncle Edgar into fast action or fast talking. She had learned to wait patiently, or sometimes impatiently, while he turned over even the simplest question in his mind before he drawled out his slow, thoughtful answer. "Course you did the right thing, Pet," he said with finality. "What other choice did you have?"

"Yeah, I guess you're right." She had already known she'd had no other choice, but it made her feel better to hear someone else back her up.

Just then a door opposite them burst open. In strode the most handsome man JoNell had ever seen in her entire life. She caught her breath at the magnificent sight of him. Latins are fantastic looking, she thought, and her skin tingled with unexpected electrified excitement.

A fierce, commanding countenance gazed down at her. JoNell saw flared nostrils, a neatly trimmed black mustache, dark green eyes, light olive skin and wavy black hair. This man had to know he was good looking, she thought. His self-confident stride announced to the world that he knew what he wanted, and he was used to getting it.

"*Aqui,*" he called over his muscular shoulder to a much smaller man who followed him into the room. He waved his arm authoritatively.

"I am so sorry for the delay," he apologized in impeccable English. His almost imperceptible bow told JoNell that here was a polished man who knew all the courtesies of high society, but refused to give them more than grudging acknowledgement.

"I am Jorge Del Toro."

Nerves jangled in remote recesses of JoNell's body. Of course. She should have recognized him from his pictures in the gossip magazines. But she hadn't expected Del Toro to meet them at the airport—and in real life he was even more dashing and handsome than in the pictures. She felt her knees turn to jelly, and for a moment she didn't think her legs had the strength to stand up.

No wonder women fell under his spell!

11

His smartly styled Italian suit hugged his tall, muscular body with just a hint of suggestiveness. His steely, cold green eyes evoked a challenge to turn his impenetrable gaze into smoldering desire. The woman who could create a look of passion in those haughty eyes must surely think herself a goddess. But that woman would be asking for heartbreak, JoNell knew. From what she'd read and heard about the man, he'd allow a woman to awaken the fires that burned under his cool exterior, sweep her to heights of romance most women only dream about, and then, when the fires cooled, dispose of her without a twinge of compassion. At least, that was what the gossips said about him.

"Welcome to my country," he said.

Uncle Edgar arose from the sofa slowly and pulled JoNell by the hand after him. "Why, thank you," he replied.

"The customs man will take care of getting you checked into the country." Then, without really looking at JoNell, Del Toro said, "What a beautiful daughter you have."

JoNell suppressed a smile. How typical of the Latin macho code. Here I stand in my jump suit, my hair in braids, no makeup, and he says I am beautiful. But Latins, she knew, judged their manhood by how smoothly they could flatter a woman and by how many conquests of the heart they could make. The truth, she thought, is not in him.

"Oh—this is my niece, not my daughter," Uncle Edgar said after a typically long pause in which his slow thinking processes lurched into gear.

Del Toro looked puzzled. "Aren't you Mr. Carpenter. And is this not Miss Carpenter?"

"Well, yes and no," Uncle Edgar replied slowly.

"Maybe you'd better explain. Why don't we all sit down?"

"Well," Uncle Edgar drawled, "Mr. Carpenter took sick."

The tale would be long in the telling. Uncle Edgar just couldn't be hurried. But JoNell didn't have the composure to shorten the tale by interrupting. She was too tired and too upset by the whole situation. Her father had suffered a heart attack brought on by business pressures. Airplane sales had fallen off, there hadn't been as many flying students, and expenses were going through the roof. With one year left in college before she earned her teaching degree, JoNell was still dependent on her parents for financial support. When she found out that this airplane sale to the wealthy South American industrialist, Jorge Del Toro, would pull them out of the woods, at least temporarily, she had insisted on ferrying the plane to Peru herself. She had met all of her father's objections. First, her mother couldn't deliver the plane because she had to take care of JoNell's father. Second, JoNell wouldn't be going alone. She would take Uncle Edgar with her. He could return home by commercial plane after the plane was delivered. And she would be well taken care of in Peru. Del Toro had already made arrangements to house JoNell and her father. Part of the deal in selling the plane to Del Toro was that he would be given some preliminary flying lessons. After the lessons were completed, JoNell could fly home by commercial plane. And finally, JoNell spoke excellent Spanish, having played as a child with Cuban refugee children and having been partly raised by a Cuban housekeeper while her parents were busy with their airplane company.

Uncle Edgar was laboriously explaining the part of the story about why he was here in his brother's place when Del Toro interrupted impatiently. "Then you, señor, are to give me the flight instructions instead of your brother?"

There was a long pause. "No," said Uncle Edgar slowly, "I just fix planes. I don't fly them."

Del Toro looked baffled. "But part of the agreement was that I was to be given flight instructions when the airplane was delivered."

JoNell struggled to hold back her laughter. Wait until he heard about the new arrangement!

"Oh, you're goin' to have the flight lessons, just like we promised," Uncle Edgar assured him. "JoNell, here, is going to be your instructor."

For a moment Del Toro was speechless. "What?" he asked incredulously. His penetrating green eyes swung in her direction and impaled her.

JoNell threw her head back with a haughty smirk. She wasn't surprised at his reaction. Of course a Latin man with his macho self-image would be shocked at the prospect of taking flight instructions from a woman. But she stood her ground and met his gaze with cool self-composure. She was not about to become apologetic, just because this man was rich, handsome, conceited and used to ordering men around and having his way with women. His reputation and his overwhelming personality did not intimidate her. When she made up her mind about something, she was as stubborn as they came. She had delivered the plane and she would give the instructions.

"I'm a very good flight instructor," JoNell said calmly.

"But you're a mere girl!" Del Toro laughed. A wave of his hand dismissed her as inconsequential.

JoNell's brown eyes flashed with rage. She had expected him to resist being taught by a woman. But to dismiss her as a "mere girl" was infuriating.

"Look, Mr. Del Toro," she snapped, rising to her full five feet, five inches. "I don't like this any better than you do. I didn't want to come here. My father took sick, and I came in his place. There's nothing in the sales agreement that says your instructor has to be a man."

"Just what qualifications do you have, señorita?" demanded Del Toro, an angry flush rising from his collar.

"Well, I've logged over a thousand hours in the air and I hold an instructor's rating for one thing," JoNell retorted. "As a matter of fact, I learned to fly an airplane before I learned to drive a car. I grew up around airplanes. I can fly them, gas them up, and even make some repairs. I may look young to you, señor, but I know what I'm doing."

Del Toro was frowning darkly, his eyes unrelenting. "Flying is serious business," he snapped.

"I know that," she retorted.

He shook his head, "You're a mere child, my dear," he insisted.

"I happen to be of legal age—twenty-one," she said angrily, "hardly a child. I'm a senior in college—"

He interrupted, "No—no. It's out of the question. I didn't bargain for this when I bought the plane. Other arrangements have to be made. I cannot accept delivery of the airplane under these circumstances—"

JoNell looked hopelessly at Uncle Edgar, but realized she wasn't going to get a whole lot of help from him. He was laboriously trying to sort out the rapid-fire dialogue.

This was a serious situation. Her parents needed to make this sale. And Del Toro was entitled to flight instruction with delivery of the airplane; that was in the contract. Possibly some arrangement could be worked out with a local flying instructor—but JoNell felt too stubbornly angry to settle for a compromise like that. First he had angered her by his infuriating manner of treating her as a "mere child." Then he was insulting her by inferring that she wasn't a competent pilot.

Impulsively, JoNell exclaimed, "If you doubt my

qualifications to fly, I'll give you a sample ride right now. Then you can judge for yourself!"

Del Toro stiffened. Her suggestion obviously took him by surprise. For the first time since he'd walked so self-assuredly into the room, he appeared to be at a loss for words. She glimpsed a strange conflict in his eyes.

JoNell pursed her lips, and tilted her head slightly to one side, as her brown eyes studied him challengingly. "What's the matter, señor?" she asked softly. "Are you afraid?"

For a long moment, a dropped pin would have rattled loudly in the deathly silence.

Del Toro's gaze flicked in the direction of the other two Latin men in the room, the customs inspector and the hangar manager who had greeted JoNell and her uncle. They were watching and listening avidly.

Del Toro looked at JoNell again. His demeanor was haughty. "Afraid, señorita? Don't be ridiculous!"

JoNell suppressed a giggle. *Ah, señor, but don't I detect a slight paleness in your cheeks? If you ask me, you're scared but you'd die before your Latin macho ego would admit it in front of these other men. . . .*

JoNell felt a moment of heady triumph. "Then, come on. I'll give you a sample of how well a woman can fly."

She led the way out the door, through the hangar and angrily jerked open the door of the Cessna. The customs man helped her remove the luggage. He promised to process it while they were in the air. Fine, she thought grimly. No flying projectiles sailing around the cabin when she proved her skill to Del Toro.

He climbed silently in beside her. A quick jerk of her head tossed her long, blond braids over her shoulders. "Better buckle your seat belt," she warned, enjoying a situation where she could give *him* orders.

She stretched out a slender hand to the ignition key. Two white tennis shoes pressed firmly on the brakes.

16

Her strong, determined voice called "Clear!" out the side window. The Cessna's engine sprang into life, and with its roar, the propeller became a spinning circle.

JoNell completely ignored Del Toro as she called the tower and received permission to taxi.

With a deft touch, JoNell inched the plane forward. It rolled smoothly. She eyed the ground traffic and headed toward the designated runway. Fortunately, the drizzle had dissipated and the sun had come out. The ground was beginning to dry. Stopping short of the runway, JoNell pushed hard on the brakes and revved the plane up to cruising speed, checking both magnetos, making sure all instruments were operating, while working up her nerve to give the haughty Del Toro the surprise ride of his life.

"Hold on," she warned through clenched teeth. She rolled out on the runway, lined the nose of the plane up with the white stripe running down the center of the pavement, and shoved in the throttle. The plane sprang forward eagerly. JoNell pushed forward on the stick, operated the rudders back and forth to steady the plane, and waited for that special feeling that always gave her a giddy shiver, the moment when the plane reached flying speed and she could sense that it wanted to make its leap into the air. At that precise moment, JoNell felt so exhilarated, she could almost have forgiven Del Toro his rudeness. She pulled back on the stick and the plane pulled away from the runway.

There was always magic in that moment. The ground fell away under JoNell and the runway shrank into a smaller and smaller ribbon. There was a freedom in the air that she could never recapture on the ground. She felt she could go anywhere, do anything, be anybody, so long as she was flying high above the dwarfed structures on the ground.

"Well, Mr. Del Toro, now do you admit I can fly a

plane? I happen to be the person who flew this airplane all the way from Florida. Uncle Edgar is a mechanic; he doesn't fly, you know."

Del Toro was sitting stiffly beside her. "But you are a woman," he said stubbornly. "It takes a man to handle a plane in an emergency—a man to instruct properly."

JoNell went momentarily blind with anger. *You never give up, do you? Well, you asked for it. . . .*

Without warning, she rammed in the throttle all the way and pulled back hard on the stick. The plane went into a steep climb. When the altimeter read 3,000 feet, she suddenly cut the throttle and pulled back all the way on the stick. The plane slowed, began to slip backward, and then nosed downward into a stall. The earth rotated into view. The plane picked up speed in its dive toward the earth. There was no sound from the engine, only the rush and whine of the wind around them.

JoNell shot Del Toro a glance. His teeth were clenched, his jaws knotted. He gripped his seat belt with knuckle-white hands. His green eyes were wide and his forehead gleamed with perspiration. But he didn't utter a sound.

Poor guy must be scared stiff, she thought. She almost relented, then remembered how he had wounded her pride, letting her know that she was a "mere girl," incapable of really flying an airplane.

JoNell watched the earth rushing toward them at a breathtaking clip. She eased in the throttle, and when she felt the plane regain control, she gently eased the plane into a level position.

She climbed back to her former altitude and put the plane into another stall. But this time, as the earth rotated into view, she gave full right rudder and right aileron and the earth did corkscrew turns as they sped toward it.

Aerobatics were not JoNell's favorite pastime. When she initiated a stall or executed barrel rolls, she always developed a quivering stomach. Trick stunts were better left to daredevil types. But she had learned all those stunts well, and now she was glad she had braved her queasy feelings.

JoNell pressed her left foot against the left rudder and turned the yolk collar, which she still called a stick, back to a more neutral position and the spinning plane slowed. When she added the throttle, the dizzying ride came to a stop, and the plane once again cruised upright over the earth.

Del Toro's olive complexion was definitely pale. She could see a pulse throbbing in his muscular neck.

Should I, she asked herself? *Why not,* she replied. *Here goes!* She gave the plane full throttle, pushed forward on the stick to keep the nose of the plane level and shoved the rudder and aileron into position. The plane sped forward. JoNell and Del Toro were mashed into their seats with crushing force. The earth turned upside down, came into view, then disappeared as the plane did a complete barrel roll, then another.

"Well," she called over the roar of the engine. "How do you like your ride so far?"

"Delightful," he managed through clenched teeth.

She righted the plane and headed back to the airport. She was feeling twinges of guilt for giving Del Toro what had probably been the fright of his life. After all, it had been a shock to him to find his life entrusted to a woman when he had expected a man. Latin men expected their women to be demure and domesticated. They were unaccustomed to the more independent women in the United States.

Well, he wasn't just a pompous stuffed shirt, all front and no substance, she had to admit. It had taken real courage to get in the plane with her when he was obviously nervous about flying. Either that or he had so much pride that he'd risk his neck before showing a weakness in public.

"I guess I should apologize," she admitted. "I had no business doing that—scaring you that way. I just wanted to prove to you that I can really fly. And I guess I was more than a little mad."

"You did scare me," he confessed. "But it wasn't what you did as much as it was having a woman flying the plane."

"You're impossible!" exploded JoNell.

Stubborn brown eyes clashed with cold green eyes. JoNell was so furious she could no longer speak. The two of them rode in stony silence back to the airport. As soon as she'd parked the airplane, she flung open the door, leaped out, and stormed into the office where Uncle Edgar was waiting for her.

"He's impossible!" she blurted out on the verge of tears. But she knew Del Toro was close behind her and she bit her lip, forcing back the tears. It wouldn't do for Mr. Superior to see her reduced to tears. That would be just the kind of evidence he needed to convince himself that JoNell was, indeed, a "mere girl."

Uncle Edgar got his large body to its feet faster than JoNell had seen in years. He strode to her side and put a comforting arm around her. "What did he do?" he demanded.

Then a strong hand touched her bare arm. Fire and ice shot through JoNell. Her arm flamed where Del Toro's fingers brushed her arm.

"I'm afraid I insulted your niece," Del Toro said, "and I owe you both an apology, señor, señorita." His bow was Latin elegance polished to perfection. "Miss Carpenter proved quite satisfactorily that she can pilot an airplane. I guess it wouldn't hurt to take a few lessons from her."

The cold, hard glint in his green eyes had vanished. Something else, quite unfathomable, had taken its place.

In spite of his patronizing, superior, macho attitude toward her—referring to her as a "mere girl"—he now was willing to concede that she knew how to handle an airplane. At least he was big enough to give that much to her.

"I'll send my car for you," Del Toro said. He shook Uncle Edgar's hand. Then he turned to JoNell and took her hand. He bent over it, and his lips brushed her fingers. Her arm was limp and her fingers burned where his lips had touched.

But when he raised his head, his green eyes met hers and the expression of amused scorn was clearly visible again. His sudden cordiality was a surface gesture. He was mocking her, and he wanted her to know it! He would stick to his part of the bargain, accepting her as his flying instructor, but he would continue to look on her as no more than an amusing child.

He's insufferable, she thought. An ego as big as his should be stuffed and put on display in a museum. I despise him. I'll give him his darn flying lessons because we need the money and then take the fastest plane back home!

Del Toro gave a perfunctory parting bow, then turned and strode from the small airport office.

The door opened again almost immediately and a short, round man who wore a waxed mustache bounced in. He bowed graciously over a rotund stomach. "Miguel Sanchez, *a su servida.*"

"That means 'at your service,'" JoNell translated.

"The car," Miguel indicated with a gesture.

JoNell and Uncle Edgar walked out ahead of the chauffeur to a long, black limousine. Miguel leaped ahead of them, swept open the back door with a flourish. The seat was filled with red roses. Miguel smiled broadly, his chubby face aglow. *"Las rosas—* they are for the señorita."

JoNell sucked in her breath. Delight swept through her. For a moment she was speechless, then she gasped, "There must be dozens!"

"You like, señorita?" Miguel beamed.

"Oh, yes. I adore flowers!" she exclaimed.

Obviously, they were a gift from Del Toro, arranged as a welcoming gesture when he thought she was to be a guest in his home while her father taught him flying. The flowers had no personal meaning. They were simply a matter of Latin protocol. He'd probably had a secretary take care of the matter, and he might not even remember he had left orders for the flowers to be delivered. Never mind; she'd enjoy the flowers for themselves.

JoNell scrambled into the back seat, exclaiming over the huge bouquet. "Why, there must be a hundred roses here, Uncle Edgar," she sighed. "I've never seen anything like it!"

"Pretty near fills up the back seat, doesn't it?" Uncle Edgar observed.

Miguel twirled the pointed ends of his mustache, bowed again, then scurried around to the driver's seat.

JoNell picked one of the long-stemmed roses from the array and sniffed the sweet fragrance.

The ride to Del Toro's estate was delightful compared to her encounter with the arrogant Del Toro. Miguel entertained them with funny stories in his broken English mixed with Spanish. When necessary, JoNell translated for Uncle Edgar.

Miguel drove like a maniac. JoNell giggled nervously, thinking that she had felt safer flying through the pass in the Andes at 13,000 feet! Everyone drove like that in Peru, Miguel explained. Through the window,

JoNell saw other drivers wildly cutting in front of each other, making sudden, tire burning stops at red lights, waving angry fists and calling insults at each other. But in spite of all the emotional confrontations on the road, Miguel assured JoNell and Uncle Edgar that Peruvians had very few wrecks. Most of the cars on the road were older models since automobiles were quite costly in Peru. So the local citizens were careful not to bang up their prized transportation.

As Miguel took them through the city, JoNell was conscious of the contrast between colonial architecture and modern skyscrapers. For several blocks they drove on wide avenues, then suddenly turned into narrow side streets and were transported into the sixteenth century when Peru was a Spanish colony. They passed houses with Spanish balconies and plazas with their dominating churches. JoNell had read a number of books on Peruvian history before this trip. She knew a great earthquake had destroyed half the city in 1746. When Viceroy Amat arrived in 1761, he had brought with him architects to rebuild the city, and during that period, colonial art had flourished.

JoNell saw stucco walls surrounding buildings and homes. Arch-shaped passageways in the walls gave entrance to patios where banana trees and other tropical plants grew in lush profusion.

They turned down the tree-lined Avenida de Descalzos which lead to the convent of the same name.

Miguel pointed out one of the tourist attractions, the Quinta de Presa. It was a beautiful rococo palace built under the influence of Viceroy Amat, and now was a museum. JoNell made a mental note to visit the building if she had the opportunity to do some sightseeing while she was in Lima.

At last they left the main part of the city behind and arrived at the residential suburbs. Miguel drove the big car through a gateway, followed a winding graveled drive under a thick grove of trees and finally arrived at a large parking area outside a bright yellow garage. Beyond the garage was a colonial style two-story home that could only be described as a mansion. The estate grounds were on a bluff and from this vantage point there was a view of the blue Pacific sparkling in the distance.

"We are here," Miguel announced with an obvious note of pride. He jumped out of the front seat, hurried around to JoNell's side of the limousine and opened her door with a deep bow.

"Señor Del Toro tell me to say for him, *Mi casa es su casa.* My house is your house."

Chapter 2

"I show you to your rooms, then I bring your bags," Miguel said. He took JoNell's hand, helped her out of the back seat, then opened the door for Uncle Edgar. He showed the way along a graveled path that wound between shrubbery from the parking area to the mansion. "You be very *cómodo* here. You like it?"

JoNell sensed that it was extremely important to Miguel that she be pleased. "Oh, yes. It's beautiful," she said with total honesty. The great mansion was yellow stucco with black, wrought-iron filigree over the windows. The massive lawn was immaculate, not a blade of grass out of place. In the center of the yard, in front of the mansion, a water fountain bubbled and splashed. Along the stucco fence were trees, shrubs and flowers. Wild orchids grew in profusion. A greenhouse tucked back under the trees was as large as JoNell's little home back in Florida. A large balcony jutted out from one side of the house, under which was a sun deck. Behind the house was an Olympic size swimming pool.

"Come inside," Miguel urged, opening a massive oak front door.

The interior of the house was magnificent. A marble floored foyer led directly to an outdoor patio with another dazzling lighted fountain. The entire house was built around the patio, and all rooms opened onto it. High ceilings gave the rooms an air of spaciousness. Floor to ceiling windows were draped with red velvet. Expensive paintings gave a special touch of elegance to the walls. JoNell recognized an original Goya and a Rembrandt. Sparkling chandeliers hung from the high ceilings. White doves cooed inside golden cages on each side of a white marble statue of Venus. On one side of the main entrance room was a cage-like door which JoNell realized opened to an elevator.

"Nice, huh?" Uncle Edgar finally commented.

"I'd say that's an understatement," JoNell gasped. "Do real people actually live in houses like this?"

"I dunno," replied Uncle Edgar. "But it appears we're about to find out."

"This way, *por favor*," Miguel said with a slight bow. "I show you your rooms."

"Well, thank you," drawled Uncle Edgar, with his almost-smile pulling at his lips.

Miguel led the way up a curved marble stairway. He stopped at a door and opened it for JoNell. "You like?" he asked, his eyes twinkling.

JoNell stared. She had never seen anything like it in her entire life. A huge bed with a red velvet canopy matching the bedspread dominated the room. The walls were lined with baskets of red roses. The dressing table was topped with red roses. In fact, the entire room was a sea of red roses.

"Oh!" JoNell squealed. "I can't believe it. Are all those flowers for me?"

"Si, señorita. They are a gift from señor Del Toro."

Some of JoNell's elation evaporated. Of course Del Toro had ordered the flowers before he met JoNell. He had had the roses placed in her room when he thought she was coming to Peru with her father, wanting to be the elegant and expansive host of the *Americano* fliers. Now, after discovering JoNell was going to be his instructor, and after the way she had tricked him into the airplane and then scaring the living bejabbors out of him, he probably wished he'd had the room filled with stinkweeds!

"I bring your luggage right away," Miguel said. He disappeared down the hall with Uncle Edgar.

JoNell pushed unpleasant thoughts about Jorge Del Toro out of her mind and dashed from basket to basket, hugging huge armfuls of flowers, drinking in their fragrance. Once she caught sight of herself in a mirror and giggled. Her casual braids, blue jump suit and white sneakers were definitely out of place in all this opulence.

A knock at the door signaled that Miguel had arrived with her bags. "Dinner is at ten, señorita," he said in Spanish.

"Thank you," JoNell replied in the same language. "Uncle Edgar and I will be there."

Miguel's round face lighted up in obvious amusement. He set the bags down and left.

What was so funny? Her Spanish wasn't that bad. Her Cuban friends back home told her she spoke like a native. Perhaps Miguel too was amused at how silly she looked in her scruffy flight clothes amidst all these elegant roses.

The first order of business was a hot bath. JoNell found the adjoining bathroom. It had white plastered walls, a sunken blue tile tub and a rich blue rug on the marble floor. On the dressing table was a small portable color TV. JoNell flipped it on.

Slender fingers turned on the gold hot water knob, sending billows of steam into the air. JoNell unzipped her one-piece jump suit and let it fall around her fragile ankles. How wonderful it would feel to wash away the grime of travel. She had plenty of time for a long, hot soak in the tub. Next, she removed the rubber bands which held her thick braids and shook out her wavy hair letting it fall in a golden cascade down her back. The steam would loosen the design imprinted by the plaits and make her hair softly manageable. She dumped a generous amount of bubble bath into the tub, tested the water with her toe, and then slid into the billowing suds with a happy sigh.

For a taste of this luxury, she supposed she could tolerate Jorge Del Toro for a while. After all, she had braved types like him before in her father's business. Some of those rich businessmen who had come to her parents for flying lessons were almost as boorish as Del Toro. They threw their money around and thought it would buy them special privileges with the instructor's daughter. She had decided long ago that men with money and power never learned to develop themselves as compassionate human beings. They figured they could buy their way through life. And Jorge Del Toro was certainly no exception. However, he had the added threat of a brooding handsomeness that gave him a double-edged power with women. His wealth, power, self-assurance, incredible good looks, all combined with the remote coldness in his eyes, was a challenge that few women could resist.

And I'm a woman, JoNell thought with a momentary stab of uneasiness as she pictured the intimacy of the airplane cockpit, with just the two of them cruising at romantic altitudes. A perfect place for him to try to trap her into wanting to fire the mysterious cold green depths of his eyes with desire.

She blushed and silently chided herself for the direction her thoughts had taken. She could rest easy! The cold steel in Del Toro's eyes was not intended to ensnare her. He saw her as a mere girl, certainly not in the class of a jet set playboy, and one that had caused him a great deal of irritation at that!

JoNell's reverie was interrupted by a vague, uncomfortable feeling. A gnawing in the pit of her stomach was growing more insistent. Ah, yes, that was her stomach crying out for food. In her excitement, she had forgotten that it was a Peruvian custom to eat a very late dinner. She had failed to nibble on a snack to tide her over until the late evening meal was served. Her mouth watered at the thought of exotic, foreign cuisine in an authentic atmosphere. The foreign cooking promised an exciting experience almost equal to the flowers she had received.

JoNell reluctantly lifted her revived body from the warm, sensual caress of the tub and toweled until her body glowed a healthy pink. Then she opened her suitcases for the first time and shook out her traveling wardrobe which consisted of several jump suits of different colors, a sweater, a light jacket, and three dresses. While she realized that pants on women were not as acceptable in Peru as they were back home, she had anticipated that most of her time would be spent with Del Toro in the airplane, and jump suits were the most practical attire. Just in case, however, she had packed one party dress. Her slender fingers caressed the black chiffon. Now she was glad that she'd had the foresight to include the party dress.

Regardless of what Del Toro thought of her, JoNell was determined to give him those flying lessons. However, it would be more pleasant if he didn't continuously regard her with that superior, impatient smirk, as if she were nothing more than a stubborn, willful child.

JoNell slipped the dress over her head and pulled its tight waist line down to hug her small middle. When she sat down, the draping fabric outlined slender, well-proportioned thighs, and a tight, compact set of hips. Her high breasts filled out the bodice nicely. The v-neckline hinted of voluptuous curves just begging to be seen, but in fact, it revealed nothing to view. Just let him call me a "mere girl" after he sees me in this, JoNell thought contemptuously. Black satin pumps with ultra high heels and a pearl necklace completed the picture of simple elegance.

Dressed in black, she looked years older and almost seductive, she knew. But there was a problem with her hair. The fluff of blond curls tumbling about her shoulders said "model" or "actress" or maybe even "show girl." While she was tempted to see if her appearance would turn on a light in those cold, steely green eyes of her host, she decided that her main objective was to convince Del Toro she was a woman, not a girl. A flick of her deft fingers placed her hair in an elegant knot on the top of her head. A single red rose, pinned on the left side above the ear, completed the look she was striving for.

She checked out the effect critically in a full length mirror. Full, almost pouting lips, a pert nose and long lashes were reflected. Yes, she decided, she would go the full route and put on mascara, a hint of rouge and frosted lipstick. Her creamy complexion needed no foundation, so she patted on a dab of powder to soften the sheen on the tip of her small nose.

She had just finished when she heard a heavy rapping on her door.

"You ready, pet?" drawled Uncle Edgar's voice.

"Yes," JoNell called. "I'm coming."

"I'm starved—" Uncle Edgar began, but stopped in mid-sentence. "Why, I never—" he blurted out. "My land, child. You're not a child anymore. You've gone and grown up on me. Overnight."

JoNell's heart purred, pleased at Uncle Edgar's reaction. Just wait until Del Toro sees her. Quite a contrast from the pigtailed girl in the jumpsuit!

They walked down the long hall, arm in arm, certainly a contrasting "odd couple," JoNell in her sophisticated black chiffon party dress and high heels, and Uncle Edgar ambling along in his wrinkled, out-of-style suit that was a good inch short of covering his bony wrists.

"I'll be leaving early in the morning," he told her. "Miguel is driving me to the airport. Do you want to come along to see me off?"

She squeezed his arm affectionately. "You know I wouldn't miss it."

They descended the stairs and turned down the hallway to large double doors. "This must be the dining room," JoNell concluded, hearing voices. Uncle Edgar opened the doors.

A hush fell over the room. JoNell was surprised to see fifteen or twenty people standing to the left of a long dining table which was situated under a massive glass chandelier. She had expected a small dinner with just Del Toro and perhaps one of his lady friends. Invisible mice nibbled nervously at her stomach.

Some forty pairs of eyes swung in her direction. For a moment, a feeling of panic touched her. But her nervousness eased when Del Toro moved away from the others to greet them.

"I hope we're not late," JoNell apologized in Spanish. She stood tall, her neck arched like a proud swan. Large brown eyes searched steely green eyes for a reaction. Fire bit JoNell's cheeks as she saw amusement dance across Del Toro's perfect features. Mixed with the amusement was a curious glint in his eyes.

A strong, masculine hand reached for her fingers. Momentarily, JoNell was electrified by the sight of Del Toro, with his nostrils flaring, his hard green eyes sending shivers down her spine. He looked absolutely devastating in his immaculately tailored black dinner jacket set off with one bright red rose in the lapel. No wonder he was a lady killer! He might be a complete wash-out in the personality department, but those devilishly good looks would set any woman's heart aflutter. As impervious as JoNell felt herself to be to his artificial charms, she felt uneasy about spending much time in the presence of such a dashing man. But then she remembered his rude, supercilious manners and assured herself that any advances from him would be easy to rebuff, regardless of his good looks.

"Your timing is perfect," Del Toro assured her in English with a sweeping bow.

His large hand lifted her delicate one to his lips. JoNell's flesh stung where he planted a lingering kiss on the back of her fingers. Oh, I get it, she thought; Mr. Personality saves all of his charm for public displays. She remembered how brusque he had been with her at the airport, how perfunctory his manners had been there. But now he had an audience. What a hypocrite, she thought!

Del Toro, the perfect, suave host, moved toward the dinner table. His firm hand gripped JoNell's left elbow. "You look stunning," he said huskily.

"Like a woman?" JoNell demanded her victory. "Not a 'mere girl'?"

"Very definitely like a woman," Del Toro conceded.

The upward thrust of JoNell's tapered chin signaled triumph. But the hard squeeze of Del Toro's fingers biting into the soft flesh of her arm unnerved her. Had she overplayed her hand? She was definitely not throwing herself into the ring to be one of Del Toro's playthings, to be toyed with, then made to suffer after she had lost the battle. Her only purpose was to make Del Toro take her seriously.

"You are to sit next to me," Del Toro commanded. He led JoNell to her chair, pulled it out for her and waited until she was seated. The other guests were sitting around the long table. Uncle Edgar was relegated to a place near the far end of the table. JoNell's concern for her uncle was relieved when she saw his "almost-smile" as he chatted with a guest who obviously spoke English.

JoNell found herself seated across the table from a petite, demure young woman in her early twenties. Her simple but elegantly styled gown and the jewelry that twinkled on her fingers and wrist gave her an air of family wealth.

"Permit me to introduce Consuelo Garcia," Del Toro murmured.

The pale-skinned young woman lowered her eyelashes in apparent embarrassment. The blue veins beneath her delicate complexion throbbed noticeably. Shyness must have kept her tongue immobile, for she said nothing to JoNell. A flush spread over her milkwhite cheeks.

JoNell felt a chilly draft in the air. An expression of hidden amusement in Del Toro's eyes told her there was something going on here that she did not understand. She felt uncomfortable, and he seemed to sense that and enjoy it.

No point in getting tangled in Del Toro's little web of a joke, JoNell told herself. Instead, she glanced in the direction of the other guests. She felt out of place here, but it was more than just being in a foreign country with strangers. JoNell didn't fit in; there was a kinship among these people that excluded her.

Her gaze fell on the huge diamond worn by the man seated next to her. Everywhere she looked, she saw elegant clothes, genuine diamonds and gold. Only she wore costume jewelry. Of course she felt like an outsider in this circle of the super rich.

Then the sumptuous Peruvian meal was served, and JoNell temporarily forgot about being self-conscious. First there was a fish appetizer, *escabeche*. Then a soup course, *chupe de camerones*, made of potatoes, milk, shrimp, hot chili peppers and eggs. The main course was duck served with steaming rice. And a second meat course were *anticuchos*, the shish kebab of South America which consisted of beef hearts served on a skewer and dipped in piquant sauce. For dessert, there was *arroz con leche*, more rice, which seemed so popular on Peruvian tables, cooked until soft, sweetened and then topped with raisins, orange rind and cinnamon. A large bowl of black-skinned fruit JoNell had never seen before was served with dessert. Several kinds of fine wine added their touch of elegance to the meal.

At one point, JoNell glanced up into a pair of glacial green eyes. "You're not eating," she said to Del Toro.

His full mouth twisted into a mocking grin. She saw that amused twinkle in his eyes again.

"What is so funny?" she demanded hotly.

"Your Spanish."

"And just what is wrong with my Spanish?" she demanded. "I speak quite fluently."

"Yes, that is true. But you talk like a Cuban. You swallow your s's. Do you know how amusing it is to encounter an American who talks Spanish like a Cuban?"

"Is that what everyone finds so amusing?"

"Yes, my little Cuban Flower," he said with that infuriatingly superior, mocking note in his voice.

"I am not your 'little Cuban Flower'!" JoNell felt an angry flush sting her cheeks. "I am not your little anything!"

"You're my little flight instructor," Del Toro corrected.

"Why can't you take me seriously?" Anger made a pulse in her temple throb.

"You want me to take you seriously? All right." With a silver spoon, he tapped a crystal goblet bearing the initials "JDT." A sudden hush fell over the room.

Del Toro pushed back his chair and arose. "Ladies and gentlemen," he began in Spanish, "I want to introduce to you my special guests for the evening." He repeated his remarks in English, obviously for the benefit of Uncle Edgar. At least he had a modicum of genuine courtesy, thought JoNell.

He introduced Uncle Edgar to the guests first. JoNell decided that his male macho background had taught him that men were more important than women. Then his gaze fell on JoNell. She felt a shiver from his penetrating stare. "And this is JoNell Carpenter, from the United States. She is going to give me flying lessons."

JoNell sensed the curiosity in the many eyes looking her over. Were they asking, "Is she, the young *Norte Americano*, to be Del Toro's new romantic conquest?" Why else would he bring a flying instructor, a girl, from the United States? She could imagine the gossip already beginning. She felt even more self-conscious and angry. She had come here on a simple business mission, to deliver the airplane, give the flying lessons and return home. Being put on display and made a subject of gossip for Jorge Del Toro's friends was not part of the deal.

As soon as the meal was over, JoNell fled from the

room, through double doors to a veranda. Tears were stinging her eyes. She felt homesick, humiliated and angry. There had been a clash of personalities between her and Del Toro the first moment they met, and it was not getting any better. She found him insufferable. How was she going to give lessons to a man like that?

A large hand grasped her elbow. "What's the matter, Pet?" Uncle Edgar drawled.

She was so grateful for his presence, she almost melted into his arms and cried on his shoulder. But she stopped herself in time. It would never do to let Uncle Edgar know how miserable she felt. As protective as he was of her, he might insist that she forget this whole unpleasant business and return to the States with him at once. That she could not do. For one thing, she couldn't take the chance of failing to complete the sales agreement of delivering the airplane along with flight instructions. The sale was too important to her parents' business. And in addition, she had too much pride to let Del Toro's arrogant nature send her whimpering home. She had stood up to him in the beginning and she'd continue to do so in spite of how uncomfortable she might feel around his snooty friends, in spite of how they might gossip about her, and especially in spite of Del Toro's infuriating, mocking manner.

"I think I have a lash in my eye," JoNell explained to her uncle. "It really hurts. I'd better find a rest-room and see if I can get it out."

JoNell fled gratefully into the security of a bathroom off the main hallway. She was glad to see she had a vanity room to herself. A look into a mirror revealed moist, dark lashes, but fortunately, the brown mascara hadn't run. JoNell dabbed carefully at her eyes so as not to ruin her makeup.

Suddenly, the door opened. JoNell turned and recognized Consuelo Garcia, the quiet, beautiful, extremely shy girl who had been seated on the other side of Del Toro at the dinner table. JoNell tried a friendly smile. "Hello, Consuelo."

The lovely young Peruvian woman did not smile back. Instead her black eyes narrowed coldly and her lips pursed. "Leave Jorge alone!" she snapped.

JoNell was momentarily speechless. What a remarkable change had come over the pale-skinned, dark-haired girl! At the dinner table, she had been utterly demure, hardly saying a word, and apparently painfully shy. There was nothing shy or reticent about her now. Her eyes were blazing with a primitive challenge. There was metal in her voice.

"I saw the look on your face when your eyes turned to Jorge," Consuelo continued. "You might as well get those thoughts out of your head, because he's mine!"

JoNell recovered from her initial surprise. "Well that's fine with me!" she exploded. "I certainly don't want him, and I can't imagine why you think I would."

Consuelo tossed her head back, her chin raised haughtily. "I've seen that look before—that look on your face. Many times. With many women who have gazed at Jorge Del Toro that way. You think Jorge is a big challenge. You want to prove to yourself that you are woman enough to ensnare him. That's what all the women think. And he loves it. Latin men judge their masculinity by the number of women they can make fall in love with them. But it means nothing to them. It's just an ego trip to see if they can woo you and win you. And when they have you, they don't want you. They want somebody new who has yet to fall under the spell of their charm."

"I'm sure you know Latin men better than I," sighed JoNell. "But I can assure you that I have absolutely no interest in your señor Del Toro, other than giving him flying lessons."

"Maybe you *think* you don't, but I repeat—I know that look. You tell yourself you're different from other

36

women, that you won't fall for him. But I've seen it happen over and over again. Jorge and I grew up together. In that time I can't count the number of his conquests. No woman is immune to his charms. Not even you, though you may tell yourself you are."

The conversation was becoming tedious. "Look, you're wasting your breath and your time—" JoNell began.

But Consuelo interrupted, "I'm warning you. Jorge has romanced many rich and famous women. He's bored with them. But you—you're something new. You're from the common class."

JoNell felt her anger rising.

Consuelo continued, "That makes you enticing to a man like Jorge. You're a new challenge, a new type of plaything for him to have his fun with."

Consuelo's words carried an open insult. Back home, such a verbal attack would have meant nothing since the United States was a classless society. But in Peru, class distinction separated the wheat from the chaff. By referring to her as from the "common class" Conseulo implied that JoNell was far beneath Del Toro and his friends on the scale of humanity, that JoNell was mere scum from the streets. JoNell felt a mixture of anger and humiliation.

"Jorge and I are of the same breeding," Consuelo went on. "We are both from rich, established families. When we marry, our combined fortunes will start an empire in this country. You can't really think he would take a common, poor girl like you seriously?"

"Oh, you think not?" JoNell retorted. "You could be wrong—"

"Everyone's laughing at you," Consuelo smirked. "You couldn't possibly fit in with real aristocrats. You don't have the class, the polish."

JoNell thought that any moment Consuelo's pupils would lengthen into thin slits. "I may not have your money señorita," JoNell exclaimed. "But I have something you don't have. I have independence. I'm not afraid of Del Toro's charms. I have my own life to live. I'm not dependent on Del Toro to make my life complete. But you obviously are. Without him, you are nothing. Without him, I'm still me!"

Consuelo's pale cheeks were now aflame. "You think you're so smart—so independent! Just you wait. You will be alone in that airplane with Jorge. You think you can have a casual flirtation with him and go home unscathed. But he'll break your heart, just the way he's done with all the others. And you'll regret it later, when it's too late, because you'll find that no man will ever measure up. No man will ever again be able to make you happy. I'm warning you. He'll make you fall in love with him. But he will marry me!"

Chapter 3

JoNell awoke with a start. Where was she? The bright red hue of the canopy over her bed danced dizzily before her eyes. She felt groggy and strangely disoriented. A curious sense of panic began tightening her stomach. Brown eyes darted quickly around the room. When they saw a denim travel bag with a pale blue jump suit draped over the top, JoNell's momentary fright gave way to relief. Of course, now she remembered. She was in Peru.

No wonder she had reacted so intensely. In two day's time she had been transported from the United States to a foreign country, from a modest middle-class existence to the bosom of opulence. On top of that, she had had to convince the arrogant Jorge Del Toro that she was a qualified flight instructor, only to find that her utterly practical motives were being misconstrued as romantic designs on the man. It was almost enough to make her give up and return home. But not quite.

JoNell had a certain determination of heart that was not easily budged. "Stubborn," her father often called her. "Persistent," she had labeled herself, believing there was a difference. Stubbornness refused to yield to reason. But persistence—ah, that was stubbornness based on reason. In the present instance, she assured herself, she was merely being persistent. She certainly had every practical reason to stay in Peru and conclude the sales contract for her father. Even her father would have to agree that this time she was being persistent!

A tapping at the door jolted JoNell out of her reverie.

"Who is it?" she called.

"It's me," said the voice of Uncle Edgar.

"Come on in," JoNell answered, scrambling out of bed and slipping into a nylon robe.

"I found Miguel coming down the hall with your breakfast. I told him I'd bring it to you." He placed the heavy silver tray on her bedside table.

JoNell touched the rich, gleaming metal. It was solid silver, she was certain, not cheaply plated.

"Thanks," she said. "I'm really hungry. What time is it anyway?" she asked around a mouthful of dark, tasty fruit.

"It's getting late, Pet," Uncle Edgar said slowly. "I have to leave for the airport soon. I let you sleep as long as possible. You seemed mighty tired when the dinner party was over last night."

I had every reason to feel that way, JoNell thought wryly—having to defend myself against two attackers. First Del Toro, who finally conceded I could fly, and then Consuelo Garcia, who is convinced I'm the next willing victim on Del Toro's list of conquests.

"Well, I'm fine now," she assured her uncle. "I slept just great. Did you?"

"Not entirely." Concern edged his voice.

"Why not?" JoNell asked a bit anxiously. "Do you feel all right, Uncle Edgar?"

"Well, yes and no," the large-faced man answered, a weary frown creasing the deep wrinkles of his brow. "My mind feels okay. It's my heart I'm worried about."

JoNell felt color drain from her face. Maybe the trip had been too much for him. All those years of heavy drinking had to take their toll on his body.

"I'll call a doctor," she said quickly.

"Oh, no, Pet. That's not the way I mean it," he reassured her. He sat on the edge of the bed beside her and gently patted her shoulder. "Before we left home, your father made me promise not to leave you here if I thought you would be in any danger."

"Danger?" JoNell asked, puzzled. Then a smile crossed her face. "But Uncle Edgar, I'm not in any danger," she laughed.

"I'm not so sure," he slowly murmured. "I saw the way Del Toro looked at you. My head tells me you can take care of yourself. But my heart, well that's a different story. It tells me not to leave you here at the mercy of a dashing, handsome, rich foreigner. My heart tells me you're much too young and vulnerable for the likes of señor Jorge Del Toro."

"Uncle Edgar! What kind of a girl do you think I am?" she gasped.

"Last night I saw a gorgeous woman, not a girl. I'm sure Del Toro saw the same thing. You've grown up, JoNell. You're a woman now. But you're inexperienced. I've been around, as you know. And I've seen every kind of man that lives. Believe me, Pet, I've seen men like Del Toro, and they're dangerous."

"Dangerous? What do you mean?" But she knew all too well exactly what Uncle Edgar meant. She had felt the powerful attraction of Jorge Del Toro the first

40

instant she had seen him. He had a magnetic quality, a strange and fatal fascination that no woman could deny. And he could be utterly ruthless with women.

Uncle Edgar gave her a long, searching look.

"Yes, I guess I do know what you mean," JoNell finally conceded. "I felt it, too. But Uncle Edgar, he's no worse than a lot of the rich playboys who've come into the office back home. I'm used to his type. And I can handle him. Believe me."

"I don't know. I promised your father. . . ."

"It's because of father that you have to let me stay," JoNell argued. "It might kill him if this deal for the sale of that airplane falls through."

"It would surely kill him if anything happened to you, Pet," Uncle Edgar said gravely.

"Well, I'm not leaving, and that's it. I won't let Daddy down."

"But you expect me to?"

JoNell felt a wave of guilt. "Uncle Edgar, remember that young good-looking stockbroker from Miami who took flying lessons from Daddy for so long? He tried his best to make me one of his conquests. He had a lot going for him, too, where women were concerned. Remember that flashy Porsche he drove? Well, he didn't get to first base with me. And there have been others. I'm impervious to that type. I've been around enough of them to know how to take care of myself. I certainly wouldn't for one minute believe their flowery lines. Trust me, Uncle Edgar. I wouldn't let you go back without me if there was any chance that Del Toro could fool me. But he can't. I'm on to his type. And what's more, I find him insufferable. And you know how he feels about me!"

"Maybe you're right," Uncle Edgar gave in. "But I won't rest easy until you're back home and I know you're safe."

"I'll be just fine," she said firmly, wishing she felt as firm deep down. She was doing a good job of convincing Uncle Edgar. Now if she could only convince herself!

"If you'll excuse me, I'll get ready to go with you to the airport."

Uncle Edgar left JoNell to her dressing.

Soon they were speeding along in Del Toro's black Rolls Royce with Miguel at the wheel. JoNell and Uncle Edgar chatted about the plush surroundings they had been enjoying and how different life was in the upper stratum of South American society.

"As glamorous as it all is, I could never fit in," JoNell quipped with a laugh, and then had a strange, uneasy feeling. Was it because Consuelo had made such biting remarks about her middle-class background? Or was there another reason, which she, herself, did not understand?

At the airport, JoNell felt herself torn emotionally. Sudden loneliness at seeing Uncle Edgar leave coupled with an uneasy feeling at being abandoned so far from home in the company of a man like Del Toro almost prompted her to give up her stubborn plan and ask Uncle Edgar to take her home with him. But she swallowed her temporary weakness, reminding herself that she must stay if only for her father's sake. She had never let him down in any way that really mattered, and she wasn't about to start now.

JoNell waited in the observation tower until Uncle Edgar's plane faded into the horizon. She sat for a long moment, sighed deeply, then resolutely squared her shoulders. She felt like an accused primitive who had to prove himself worthy by walking over live coals. Her test of fire took the human shape of a handsome man, but it would be a grueling test all the same. She would have to continue to prove to him that she was as capable as any man to give him flying instructions, and at the same time be on guard against his overpowering charm.

On the ride home, JoNell listened with only half an ear to Miguel's running chatter. She laughed politely at his jokes and humorous observations about life, but her mind was elsewhere. Then Miguel began talking about Del Toro, and JoNell found herself paying attention.

"The señor is not what you may think," Miguel was saying. "He is a good man. He has a big heart."

"So I've heard," JoNell murmured. The irony in her voice was obviously lost on Miguel.

"The señor is really a man of the people," he said.

"So I've heard again," JoNell agreed. *All of them women!*

"It is a sad situation," Miguel continued.

For scores of broken-hearted women.

"He is really quite unhappy in some ways."

Because he doesn't have time for more women?

"He is a very generous man."

Yes—with his flowery lines.

"Most people don't know what he is really like."

Just ask his previous lovers!

"But I know a side of him no one else has ever seen," Miguel offered.

"Oh?" For some reason no sarcastic thoughts came to mind now, and she leaned forward to better hear Miguel.

"I know the real man," Miguel said in a confidential, important tone. "I am one of the few persons in the entire world who knows the real Jorge Del Toro."

JoNell waited for a long, expectant minute. But Miguel fell silent. He darted expertly in and out of the fast-moving traffic.

"Well, go on," JoNell prompted.

"I'm driving as fast as I can."

"That's not what I meant, and you know it," JoNell

43

said with a grin. "Finish what you were going to say about señor Del Toro."

"Oh, then you are interested?" A light danced in Miguel's eyes.

"Well, of course," JoNell said. "I'm going to teach him to fly. The more I know about him, the better I can teach him."

"The señor is a good man. He has been good to me and to all who work for him. He pays me very well. He paid for an operation for my youngest child, Pachia, who would have been a cripple. I owe him much."

Again Miguel fell silent. JoNell waited impatiently. When it was obvious Miguel had come to the end of what he was going to say, JoNell prompted him again.

"Go on, please."

"I think I should not. I have said too much already. The señor would not like for me to tell you about his private life."

JoNell fumed silently. Why did Miguel bring up the topic of Del Toro's private life if all he planned to do was tease her with it? No matter how she felt about the man, anyone would be eager to hear more about the private side of South America's most notorious lover. Maybe Miguel wanted to be persuaded. Perhaps he needed to feel important.

She leaned forward until her arm rested on the back of the front seat. "Miguel, I'd really like to know more about señor Del Toro. Please tell me—"

The car careened at a dizzying angle as Miguel suddenly darted from a slower lane of traffic and sped even faster down the road. Having somehow averted the total destruction of their vehicle by a matter of inches, Miguel settled down and resumed his story. "Señor Del Toro is really a man of the people. Don't let all his money fool you. Yes, he is very wealthy, but in his heart he is not truly happy in that big house day after day. So he goes to a little town in the mountains. I have relatives there. It is the señor's retreat away from the world. You don't know him as I do. I have seen him many times working in the village side by side with the poorest of men. He puts on his old clothes and goes deep into the copper mines that he owns there. He visits many poor people in the village, and he tells me to take care of their needs. He sends food and clothing.

"The happiest days the señor spends are those in the village high in the mountains," Miguel continued. "I have heard him laugh and talk with the men. I have seen him play with the children and take care of the sick. Everyone there loves him for himself. They do not love him just because he is rich. They love him because he is a good man. The señor has many charities. He has done much for the villagers. He gave money to build a school. He set up a medical clinic and pays doctors to visit the village and care for the sick. I tell you, the señor is a good man. Ask anybody who works for him. They will all tell you of the good things he has done for them. But you must never tell the señor I have told you this. He would be very unhappy with me."

"Of course," JoNell answered.

"Promise me, señorita."

"Yes, I promise, Miguel. Don't worry. I'll be here only a short time to give señor Del Toro his flying lessons. Before you know it, I'll be gone. You needn't worry that I'll let any of what you told me slip out between now and then. But thanks for telling me."

JoNell settled back in the seat. After a brief silence, Miguel began his usual stream of chatter. JoNell tuned him out for the most part, her mind busy puzzling over the things he had said about Jorge Del Toro. Did the notorious Latin playboy actually have a secret side to his character—one that included compassion and charity for the less fortunate? She ransacked her memory of the two times she had been exposed to the man, at the airport yesterday, and at dinner last night. She shook

45

her head. The picture Miguel had drawn of him just did not fit the man she had seen. Arrogance and conceit were the only two facets of his nature he had exposed to her. If there was a human, decent side to him, he kept it well hidden.

Or, was there really another side? Miguel was obviously the faithful servant, Del Toro his *patron*. Fierce loyalty often characterized such a relationship. Perhaps Miguel wanted so much for his employer, his *patron,* to fit the idealized image, that his imagination colored the truth. Maybe Del Toro did occasionally visit his mining operations to see that they were run properly. Perhaps he had donated a small percentage of the profits from the mines—money he would never miss—to build a school and a clinic in the town in order to keep his employees content to work under unhealthful, underpaid conditions. From these few facts, Miguel had imagined a lovely story about Del Toro that had nothing to do with the real man, the ruthless man.

There was also the possibility that Miguel had lied just to get JoNell's attention. He obviously couldn't stand to be ignored. Perhaps when he saw JoNell's interest perk up, he had decided that taking her into his confidence about a "secret" side to his employer's nature was a good way to hold her attention and give himself some importance.

Of course there was a third possibility. She wouldn't put it past Del Toro to have Miguel trained to deliver a glowing characterization of his employer to any young women guests. It could be part of the Latin Casanova's methods to undermine a woman's defenses.

Frustration grew in her. Whether the story was a fanciful fabrication designed by Miguel for attention, whether Del Toro had instructed Miguel to lie, or whether the story actually had some truth in it, JoNell would never find out. She had assured Miguel that she would not reveal to Del Toro what Miguel had said, and she was always true to her word.

With an impatient toss of her head, she determined to put the matter out of her mind. Whether Jorge Del Toro was a saint or a sinner, or a little of each, did not really concern her. She was no more than a minor irritation to him—an upstart American woman he had to put up with for a few days to get his flying lessons. With movie starlets, South American socialites and the beautiful Consuelo Garcia at his feet, he would hardly have any romantic interest in a girl from a middle-class American family—a girl who wore tennis shoes, jump suits and tied her hair in braids!

At the thought of Consuelo Garcia, JoNell felt a wave of compassion for the exquisitely lovely, pale girl. She must be deeply in love with Del Toro, and probably, in his way, he loved her. But what torture the poor girl was going to have to endure all her life, married to a conceited, arrogant Casanova who made a game of breaking women's hearts!

The plane was ready to taxi to the runway. JoNell sat unnervingly close to Jorge Del Toro in the tight quarters of the small airplane's cockpit. Not since she was a teenager on her first solo flight had she been so nervous in an airplane. Was it because she was in a strange country on a mission she disliked—or because she suddenly felt unsure of herself in the presence of so handsome a man?

This morning when she had assured Uncle Edgar that she was immune to the charm of jet set playboys, she had forgotten how overwhelming was the presence of this particular playboy. The cockpit fairly sizzled with an electric charge surrounding him.

Slender white fingers gripped the stick. "Like this," a thin voice instructed.

Powerful fingers of burnished bronze imitated the delicate fingers on the twin yolk collar. But the bronze knuckles turned almost white.

"Don't grip it so tightly," the thin voice admonished. "Try to be 'more relaxed." *Lower and fuller,* she ordered her voice. *You sound like a frightened high school girl on her first date.*

Slit green eyes searched large brown eyes, and JoNell felt a quiver in her throat. A shadow of a frown crossed Del Toro's handsome features, his nostrils flared perceptively, and his dark hair looked almost blue-black against his face which had paled a couple of shades lighter. He moistened his lips which had become dry.

He's as nervous as I am, JoNell suddenly realized, and the realization gave her courage. Even though his nervousness was of a different cause—the tenseness of a student on his first flight—it put them on somewhat the same level.

"Here are the brakes," JoNell explained, managing a businesslike voice. She pushed the balls of her feet on the tops of the rudder pedals. "Do everything I do. At first I'll actually fly the plane on my controls. You'll follow through on your controls. That way you'll get the feel of flying. Almost anyone can learn the mechanical motions of flying, but it takes a real feel for flying to make you a good pilot."

Del Toro took a silk handkerchief from his breast pocket, dabbed his brow and wiped the palms of his hands.

The poor guy is really petrified, she thought. Most students were nervous at first, but he was in a dreadful state. "I'm not going to do any acrobatics today," she reassured him.

He gave her a weak smile.

He'll be okay once we get in the air, she thought.

JoNell brushed back wisps of her bangs that had tumbled to her eyebrows. She hoped she looked professional enough for Del Toro to keep his mind on flying. It had been a struggle, deciding how to dress for this first flight. She feared her usual garb made her look too girlish. On the other hand, she didn't want to encourage Del Toro's predatory inclinations by appearing too desirably feminine. So, she had worn her customary jump suit to remind him that this was not a social outing. But she had compromised on the matter of her braids. Pinning her long hair atop her head and brushing on a few dabs of mascara certainly made her look older. She was aiming for a combination of clothes, hair style and makeup so she would appear older, sure of herself, but not seductive. While she had never fancied herself a beauty, she knew that her golden hair made her stand out here in Peru where blondes were highly sought after. If nothing else, her hair would make men notice her.

"I'll operate the throttle," she explained. "You concentrate on getting a feel for the stick and the rudders. Notice how light the plane feels just before it's ready to take off. You won't have to decide when you're ready to become airborn. The plane will signal you that it's ready. If you just go with the plane, relax, give yourself over to its movements, you'll get the feel of it sooner."

JoNell kept her gaze straight ahead, talking impersonally as if she were vocalizing instructions on a tape recorder.

She called the tower, taxied, took her aim down the runway, and off they went.

In spite of the tight rein JoNell had on her emotions, she couldn't help experiencing that fantastic, giddy feeling she loved when the plane actually deserted the runway. She loved practicing "touch-and-go's" just for the thrill of takeoff. That would be one bright spot in this series of lessons she would be giving Del Toro that she could look forward to.

"First, you need to learn to hold the plane in level flight," JoNell said. "Put your feet on the rudders, hand on the stick. I'll still operate the throttle."

JoNell showed him all the proper motions, then relaxed her grip. She was impressed by his keen perceptions, though not altogether surprised. Men like Del Toro, successful, incisive, supremely confident, usually grasped instruction quickly. The plane flew smoothly, even though she had, for the most part, turned the controls over to him.

"Hey, that's quite good," she remarked with genuine admiration. "Most people don't realize that flying a plane level is actually one of the hardest maneuvers. You're doing very well."

"Thank you, señorita," Del Toro replied, looking directly at her for a moment, a smile curling the tips of his black mustache.

The impact of his gaze brought a momentary quiver to the pit of her stomach, but she quickly recovered. In an impersonal manner, she asked, "Are you learning to fly for business purposes, señor Del Toro?"

"No," he replied. "For personal reasons—for pleasure—"

He appeared to have somewhat recovered from his obvious fright before takeoff, although he still seemed tense.

"Why don't we fly along the coastline?" he suggested. "The scenery there is impressive. While you're teaching me to fly, I can show you some of the sights of my beautiful country."

It seemed a reasonable request. "Okay," she agreed. "But keep the plane level. You're climbing."

"Yes, señorita," he said with a hint of mocking deference.

They flew in silence for a while. Del Toro seemed lost in thought and JoNell was occupied with checking on the plane's flight and occasionally glancing down at the scenery which was indeed impressive. The mountains and tangled jungle terrain had given way to coastal desert plains and sparkling white beaches. From the air, the Pacific was a deep emerald.

Suddenly Del Toro said quietly, "You are a most competent flying instructor, señorita. You inspire confidence. Again I must apologize for my rude behavior yesterday. I am glad you persuaded me to allow you to give me the flying lessons."

He caught her completely off guard. Had he made some kind of crude pass, tried to put his hand on her knee, or made a remark filled with sexual implications, she would have immediately known how to respond. She was prepared for *that*. But his apologetic, friendly manner left her speechless.

"Are you no longer angry with me for my rudeness when you first arrived?" he asked in English.

"N—no," she stammered, not knowing in her confusion what she felt at the moment.

Then he said, switching to Spanish, "I must tell you, señorita, that you took my breath away when you appeared at my humble dinner last night. I had trouble believing the little girl with the braids and tennis shoes was the same stunning sophisticated woman who graced my dinner table. Now I can hold back my thoughts no longer. I must tell you how beautiful you are."

With that, JoNell's thoughts were jolted back to reality. The confused warmth she had momentarily felt at his distractingly sincere apology was dispelled by a flow of ice water through her veins. She almost felt relief that he was back in character, the compulsive Latin wolf. As she had expected, the inevitable had happened. Alone with a young woman in this isolated situation, he just couldn't resist making an obligatory pass at her. And how typical to do it in Spanish, a more romantic and flowery language!

Now her defenses were in place. "Yes, I know," she said coldly, and in English. "Everyone tells me so. So I'm afraid it really doesn't flatter me to hear you say it as much as you might hope."

"You are still angry. And you mock me unmercifully to show it."

"Unmercifully, señor? Not nearly so unmercifully as you mock a trail of women that you left with broken hearts. I'm quite afraid I know all about you and your reputation with women. Unfortunately for you, I am impervious to your charms."

He chuckled softly, joining her in speaking in English now. "Surely you do not believe all the romantic gossip you hear about a rich man? I am single, JoNell. Yes, I have known some women—but not nearly so many as the gossips would like to believe or the scandal magazines invent to sell their papers. But you must believe I am sincere when I say that none of the women I have known was like you. You were like a breath of fresh air coming into my life when you stepped out of this plane yesterday."

Again she was confused, her thoughts scattered. Her breath had caught in her throat when he used her first name.

For a reason she couldn't define, her relationship with Del Toro took on a subtle new dimension. What the use of her first name had to do with it, she didn't know, except that he was less formal with her now. It had put them on a different footing, an intimacy that she did not wish to develop between her and the notorious Jorge Del Toro, and she didn't know how to put her feelings in reverse to back out of the situation.

"Of course your women were not like me," she retorted. "They were all rich. I am middle class." Consuelo had pronounced her of the common class. It was a term JoNell could not bring herself to use. Maybe to Jorge Del Toro she was of the common class. But she had a fierce pride that refused to accept Consuelo's definition.

"That's part of your attraction," said Del Toro.

JoNell bristled. Perhaps Consuelo was right! Del Toro's interest in her could be because of her background. She was a challenge to him, a new type of woman he had not toyed with before. Maybe he would find it amusing to sample a woman far beneath his station just for curiosity's sake.

"There is something different about you that is very appealing," he continued.

"It's called poverty!" she said tartly.

"Now I've offended you again. I'm truly sorry. I didn't mean it the way you took it."

"I understand what you meant, all right," JoNell said hotly. "You Latin men are all alike. Don't think because I'm from the United States, I'm ignorant of your ways. I grew up around Cubans. I know how Latin men flatter women. But it means nothing. Now, let's change the topic, shall we? I'm supposed to be giving you flying lessons, not listening to you tell me how gorgeous I am."

A black mustache twitched above a lip drawn tight between upper and lower teeth. But he did not pursue the matter any further.

JoNell had mixed feelings. True, Del Toro was a philanderer, but it was flattering nevertheless to have one of the richest, most powerful and handsome men in Peru tell her she was beautiful. A woman would have to be dead not to enjoy hearing it, even when she knew it was a pack of lies. Still, it was a dangerous game to play, enjoying that kind of flattery even for a moment, so she swept the temptation from her mind and concentrated on flying the airplane.

"Could we land on the beach below?" Del Toro suddenly asked.

"I don't know. Why would you want to do that?"

"I have something I wish to show you."

"What?" she asked suspiciously.

He smiled mysteriously. "Please. It is something I would like very much to show you. But would it be safe to land here?"

"It might be. Some beaches are smooth and hard packed, just like a runway. Let's take a closer look."

She took the controls from him. The plane banked and made a low, swooping pass over the beach. JoNell gauged the surface of the beach with a critical eye, and noticed the direction the wind was blowing the tree leaves. She bit her lip. "It looks safe enough. No driftwood or gulleys that I can see."

Del Toro nodded. "I am sure it is a good beach for landing. I have friends who fly here often to fish. They have never had any difficulty landing their planes."

"Then I guess it's okay."

She banked the plane and approached the beach again. "The wind is coming off the water. Normally, if at all possible, you land a plane into the wind. But here the wind is coming from the side, so we'll come in at an angle, sort of sideways. We call it 'crabbing' into the wind."

She spoke in as impersonal a tone as she could manage as the sparkling beach loomed before them. "You land with the power off and then use it only to control the plane." Slender fingers gripped the throttle tightly and eased it back with a control born of long experience. Had JoNell not been so expert at her maneuvers, she surely would have given Del Toro a rough landing. That was how unsettling his presence was.

"The key to a successful landing is feeling when the plane is ready to settle to the ground," JoNell explained in concise tones.

The plane descended in a smooth, controlled glide. The roar of the engine subsided as the power waned.

JoNell kept her eyes straight ahead as she explained each succeeding move. "You must line yourself up with the runway—in this case, that hard packed stretch of beach. Now put your hands on your set of controls and follow through. As we near the landing surface, pull back on the stick, like this. Watch out your side window. Keep looking at the ground. Feet on the rudders. Keep pulling back on the stick. Think of trying to hold the plane off the ground as long as possible. It will actually land itself."

For the moment, JoNell became so embroiled in her instructions that Del Toro became simply another student.

"When the wheels touch the ground, be prepared to put your feet up on the brakes and pump gently back and forth. You must keep the plane rolling in a straight line. You have to stop it, but slowly."

She felt the rumble of the landing gear. "Perfect!" she cried enthusiastically as the wheels stopped rolling and the plane came to a stop. "You're really learning fast. I'm so proud of you. You followed through like a pro."

Del Toro was again patting his forehead with his handkerchief. His hand was trembling slightly. He gave her a weak smile.

"You seem very nervous—more than most students. Do you still distrust my flying ability in spite of what you said?"

He shook his head. "I meant what I said. You have proven to me that you are extremely competent, señorita. You must pay no attention to my nervousness. It has to do with something that happened a long time ago—something I must deal with privately. It has nothing to do with you."

He really was a most confusing man. During the takeoff, he had been extremely tense, saying nothing. Once they were in the air, he had relaxed to the point that he was handing her his flowery line. But during the landing, he had become quite nervous again.

He was less of a threat to her when he was under this strain. She felt herself momentarily put aside her distrust and antagonism. In its place was concern for an overly anxious student. "I wonder why you wish to learn to fly if it makes you uncomfortable?"

He was regaining his healthy, bronze color. He shrugged. "It is nothing. It will soon pass. You see—you are doing wonders for my morale."

"I hope so. I mean, I hope the tenseness will pass. To be a good pilot, you must be relaxed."

She felt the stunning impact of his fiery gaze searching her eyes. "I am very relaxed when I am with you, JoNell," he said softly.

Her short-lived concern for him dissolved. The gates of her defense line slammed shut. "What is it you wished to show me?" she asked coldly.

"I will show you. Come, let's stretch our legs." He unbuckled his seat belt and opened his door.

JoNell did the same. Her white sneakers hit the hard packed sand. She stretched, rubbed the back of her neck, then met Del Toro near the tail of the plane.

"Well?" she asked. "Where is it?"

He towered above her. She forgot, when they were in the plane, how tall and powerfully built he was. The muscles of his broad shoulders strained at the plaid jacket he was wearing today. She felt like a Lilliputian beside him.

He was gazing at her with green eyes that smoldered with dark concentration.

"I said where is it?"

"What?"

"What you wanted to show me," she said impatiently.

"Oh, right here," Del Toro said with an expansive

56

sweep of his broad hand. He placed his fingers on her slim shoulders, gently turned her to look around at the beach, then to face him again.

She was frowning suspiciously. "I don't know what you mean."

"In front of you!" he exclaimed. "Don't you see it? A long, golden beach. And in the center of it, what? A man!"

"Is that what you wanted to show me!" she gasped. "*You?* Is that why we landed the plane?"

"But of course," Del Toro laughed, his white teeth flashing. "You have not seen the real me since you've been here. I decided it was time you took a good look. I may not be so bad as you seem to think. To begin with, am I so unpleasant to look at?"

"Well, no," JoNell confessed. In fact, Del Toro was the most handsome man she had ever seen, though she would cut off her tongue before admitting to him that she thought so.

"Are my manners repugnant?"

"Of course not," she snapped impatiently.

"Then what is it about me that you find so distasteful?" he demanded.

Distasteful? On the contrary, JoNell found Del Toro almost irresistibly attractive—on the surface. His black hair contrasting with his fiery deep green eyes and his high forehead gave him a noble appearance. His muscular body hinted at passion only dreamed of in romantic novels. His wealth and power were sufficient to attract women in the highest circles of society.

But there was more to a person than the surface veneer. There was such a thing as character. And what JoNell knew about this man's character—or lack of it!—where women were concerned did make him repugnant to her.

"This conversation has gone far enough!" JoNell said

57

hotly. "I can't see where it makes any difference whether I find you handsome or not handsome, or distasteful or not distasteful."

"It makes a difference to me—a great difference!"

"Well, not to me. I'm here to give you flying lessons. That is my only interest in you."

"But I wish to have you become more interested in me than if I were just another student, JoNell."

"What arrogance!"

"Some women love arrogance," he smiled.

"Not this woman! You're also conceited."

"That, too, can make a man attractive."

"You're impossible!"

He threw back his head and laughed. His laughter like everything else about him was big—it echoed from the dunes.

"Please," she said with angry tears. "Leave me alone! Do you have to make a conquest of every woman you meet?"

His laughter faded and he gazed at her soberly. "Why must you think of it as a 'conquest'? Can you not believe that I find you suddenly so important in my life that I must tell you so?"

"There you go, talking in Spanish again. Do you do that automatically when you start handing a poor girl your line?"

"I am sorry," he said with a slight nod of his head. "I do it without thinking. The two languages are so comfortable for me, I switch from one to the other without realizing it. Whatever language I use, I am trying to tell you how compelling you are, how much I find myself wanting you."

JoNell swallowed hard. She felt a trembling in her knees. She tried to hold onto her anger. "You met me twenty-four hours ago," she choked. "You know nothing about me. . . ."

"I know everything about you. You are very young,

58

JoNell, but surely you must know that in the important things in life, one must trust the heart, not the mind. Something deep inside gives us the message, sometimes quickly and without warning."

Fire was raging in his slashing green eyes now. He took a step closer to JoNell. A shiver of fear gripped her. Suddenly she realized how alone they were on this deserted stretch of beach. The size of Del Toro's powerful body made JoNell feel even smaller and weaker than she really was. If he decided to take her by force, she knew she couldn't stop him. What had possessed her to land in this isolated spot with the notorious Del Toro, knowing his unsavory reputation with women as she did?

Her mouth suddenly dry, she said, "We'd better go. It's getting late."

She turned to flee to the airplane, but was cut short by a strong hand gripping her upper arm. Powerful fingers bit into her flesh.

"You're hurting me!" she gasped.

"Not as much as you are hurting me," Del Toro raged. "You don't give me a chance! Your mind is made up to hate me!"

He pulled her to him. She felt the steel bands of his arms imprison her. She struggled helplessly as he mashed her to him and pressed his hard manliness against her threateningly. She twisted her shoulders, struggled and started to scream. He held her tight with one strong arm and covered her mouth with the other masterful hand.

"It won't do you any good to scream," he whispered huskily in her ear. "There is not another living soul within a hundred kilometers."

In that instant, JoNell was sure she was in the possession of the devil. Demanding green eyes bore into hers with fierce determination. Nostrils flared with passion. She felt the fight drain from her. Almost hypnotized, she became limp and fluid in his arms. Hungry lips pressed on hers. She felt the tingle of thick hair brushing against her upper lip. The half hysterical thought crossed her embattled mind that she had never before been kissed by a man with a mustache.

She was swept up in a cloud of bewilderment as her body was pulled tighter and tighter into his powerful arms and his lips became more demanding on hers. She felt hard teeth behind his lips bruise her flesh. He loosened his grip and ran his hands slowly down her spine. A tingle raced through her. Then his hands retraced their course, moved back up her spine and stopped on her shoulders. His lips reluctantly parted from hers, and he drew back.

"Was that so terrible?" he asked in a husky whisper, his eyes searching hers.

A smoldering deep in her being, in some hidden recess of her emotions, in a place so remote from her usual thoughts that she had never guessed its existence, began to ignite in an indescribable feeling that both terrified and fascinated her. Little bands of steel in all her muscles gave her a sudden strength. Her heart pounded furiously, making her dizzy. Vaguely, she knew she could break his grip and run. But she was trapped now in a snare of her own desire, and she knew, with an intensity she had never before known in her life, that she was being controlled by some inner force that brushed aside rational thought. Only her heart told her what she must do.

He said, "Destiny brought you to my life, JoNell. That is what I felt soon after I met you. . . ."

Again, he kissed her. She could feel the hard jolts of Del Toro's pulse pounding through his body. Fire burned her lips. Now she melted against him willingly. She thought she would never get her fill of the delicious nectar of his mouth. All of her senses melted into a large ball of burning desire which begged for the touch and kiss of Jorge Del Toro. Never before had she felt so alive, so vibrant, so in need. Her body ached. In her fogged state, she forgot about the many women Del Toro had had before her, and that he would toss her aside as he had them, when his fickle nature tired of her. Tomorrow would never be and yesterday had never been. There was only this place and this moment—this strip of deserted beach and this man holding her. They were man and woman at the dawn of creation.

She was enveloped in rapturous sensations begging to be fulfilled when the kiss ended. His caressing hands stopped leaving their trail of fire on her body. His breathing that had been quick and unmeasured took on a controlled quality. He loosened his grip on her and drew back. But still his eyes searched her face. "I will have you, when the time is right," he murmured, his voice unsteady. "In your hate for me, I have found a spark of passion—"

JoNell felt drained and weak. Her arms, an empty ache in them, hung limply at her sides. At first the desire that had raged in her changed into a blank feeling of nothingness, a void sensation of occupying an empty body. Then as her strength and sanity returned, she felt the hot rise of anger. Shame overtook the anger. Humiliation made her cheeks burn. She blinked hard to hold back a flood of tears.

What a cruel and calculating man he was! Older, experienced with women, he had taken advantage of her youth and innocence.

With a shocking realization, JoNell saw what a diabolical man Del Toro was, and how exceedingly dangerous he was. He had tricked JoNell in spite of her defenses against him. He had turned on in her a flood of desire so intense she would have willingly given herself to him today, here in this place, and then regretted it the rest of her life. But he had stopped short, perhaps to prove to her just how much power he really had over her. He could toy with her as he pleased because he had her under his spell now. He had proved that he could arouse her. But he was not nearly so weak as she was. While she had been his willing victim, he had been emotionally aloof the whole time, coolly measuring her responses.

JoNell was frightened. How long would it be before Jorge Del Toro carried out his threat? She loathed him more than ever. In that moment, she vowed to never again allow him to trap her into a situation where they were alone together like this. Her hate for him was her only protection. She would use it like a sword against him until she was safely out of Peru!

Chapter 4

JoNell sat alone in the airport office, staring at the flight log. She and Del Toro had flown back in icy silence. As soon as they had landed, he had dashed off to a pressing business appointment.

Now she looked at the flying time she had recorded—one hour—and could not believe the figure she had written. She had lived a lifetime this morning. How could she write down only *one hour!* But that was the actual time in the air not counting the time they had spent on the beach.

Del Toro's purchase agreement had stipulated ten hours of flying lessons. That meant she had nine more hours in the air with that man, sitting in the cramped quarters of the small plane. That would be painful for her—but safe. He wouldn't dare make any romantic overtures when they were flying.

Because of Del Toro's busy schedule, it had been necessary to spread the ten hours of flying instructions over a two-week period. JoNell's heart sank at the prospect of spending two weeks in the household of Jorge Del Toro. Her only hope was that Del Toro's demanding business schedule would keep him so occupied she could avoid him at all times except when they were flying.

Remembering the hypnotic spell Del Toro had cast over her on the beach made a shiver run through her. How glad she would be when she was safely home in Florida, a continent away from señor Jorge Del Toro!

JoNell was filing Del Toro's flight log in a cabinet when Miguel bounced into the airport office, his jolly face a circus of grins.

"Come, señorita. The señor tell me to show you some of the city. I take you to the markets and stores. You will like these places very much."

"Thank you, Miguel. I would enjoy that."

Yes, she thought, a shopping trip would be good therapy for her jangled nerves.

Miguel drove her to a section of the city between the Bolivar and Crillon Hotels, where a four block area was filled with shops specializing in Peruvian handcrafts. JoNell spent several pleasant hours browsing among displays of alpaca wool sweaters, llama rugs, Indian masks and reproductions of Inca jewelry in gold and silver. She made a few modest purchases of souvenirs to take home with her.

Miguel waited patiently in the limousine, reading a magazine. When she finished her shopping tour, he took her on a sightseeing expedition of the impressive churches of Lima. She was certain she would have nightmares after viewing the mummified body of Francisco Pizarro in the cathedral, and the thousands of bones, skulls and skeletons laid out in neat rows in the catacombs of the Church of San Francisco. Miguel was so proud of being her guide that she didn't have the heart to object, but she was enormously relieved when they were back outside in the daylight.

They were walking to the car when something quite terrifying took place.

JoNell heard a distant rumble, and the earth quivered under her feet. She uttered a cry of alarm, clutching at Miguel's arm.

He chuckled. "It is nothing, señorita. Please do not be frightened. It is just an earthquake."

"*Just* an earthquake?" she gasped.

"Oh, not a real earthquake. Just, how you call it, a tremor. We have them all the time in Peru. Nobody pays any attention."

But this unsettling experience was the last straw after everything else that had happened to her today, and JoNell felt a distinct need to lie down. "Could you take me home, Miguel? I'm suddenly very tired."

"Certainly, señorita." He opened the car door with his usual flourish.

Miguel's usual breakneck speed on the way home was stifled at several places by crowds gathered around speakers. "Politicos doing much talking," Miguel muttered, steering his way through the throng, his horn blaring impatiently. "It is the *presidente* election soon to be held."

JoNell saw giant posters of a gray haired, mustached man glaring from under bushy eyebrows. *Gustamente por Presidente* was proclaimed in foot high letters.

Miguel proceded to give her a discourse on Peruvian politics for the rest of the trip home. It seemed that Jorge Del Toro was bitterly opposed to Gustamente and was throwing his considerable influence behind the opposing candidate, Sergio Mendez de Cardova. Miguel painted a dismal picture of Geraldo Gustamente's qualifications and what would happen to the country if he were elected.

But the matter was of no importance to JoNell. She

tuned out Miguel's running chatter and dozed the rest of the way back to Del Toro's mansion.

After a four o'clock lunch of delicious hard-crusted bread, butter and tea which was waiting for her in her room, JoNell stretched out on the enormous bed and was asleep in seconds.

It was dusk when a tapping at her door awakened her.

"Who is it?" she called sleepily.

"Miguel."

"Come in, Miguel," she said, sliding off the bed and heading for the door.

The door opened and a huge white vase filled with long-stemmed roses bobbed toward her.

"For you, señorita," said Miguel's voice from behind the advancing flowers.

More flowers, and her room already looked like a rose garden in full blossom! The roses were gorgeous. She cupped her hands around a cluster of damp buds and sniffed their rich fragrance. Under any other circumstances, she would have been delighted. She did love the flowers, no matter that they did come from Del Toro. But his card that came with them made her both furious and frightened:

"A symbol of our first kiss and what is yet to come. . . ."

"What was yet to come" for reasons JoNell could not fathom did not develop into the problem she anticipated during the next two weeks. She saw practically nothing of Del Toro except for the scheduled flying times, which he kept religiously. But when he did arrive at the airport for the lessons, she could see that he was being pressed for time. He often arrived with an entourage of cars. Business-suited men and secretaries followed him across the airfield to the waiting plane. He discussed business and dictated notes up to the moment that he climbed into the airplane beside JoNell.

She could tell that he was under a strain. He looked haggard and weary. She assumed it had something to do with the presidential election that Miguel had talked about. But it was none of her business, and she had no intention of inquiring about it. She was just thankful that Del Toro was being kept too busy to follow up on the threat he had made that day on the beach, *"I will have you when the time is right. . . ."*

She had not drawn an easy breath for two weeks, worried about what kind of new trick Del Toro might have up his sleeve to trap her into another dangerous, intimate situation like that day on the beach. But, except for daily bouquets of roses accompanied by notes of apology for not being a better host, he had shown no personal interest in her. He was preoccupied during the flying lessons, and she was cold and professional.

She had come to the conclusion that love was a game, a pastime to a philanderer like Del Toro. During that first flying lesson, he'd had a little time to spare, and he had been in the company of a young woman. So, he amused himself by seeing how far his charms could get him with her.

It had meant no more to him than that, and she would be grateful forever that the moment had stopped short of her making a terrible fool of herself.

The ten hours of flying lessons were completed on schedule. JoNell was packing to leave. And none too soon. Her mother phoned her that afternoon, her voice full of worry. JoNell's father was suffering a depression. Health and business worries had pushed him to the verge of an emotional breakdown.

JoNell managed to keep her voice cheerful and reassuring. "I'm through here, and I'm arranging to catch the earliest possible commercial flight home.

Don't worry, Mom. Everything is going to be just fine. . . ."

But the minute she hung up, she burst into tears. She sat weakly on the edge of the bed.

"Señorita, what is the matter?" asked a familiar masculine voice from the direction of the doorway.

JoNell raised long, wet lashes and saw the figure of Jorge Del Toro.

"Nothing—it's a personal matter," JoNell said unsteadily, brushing tears from her cheeks.

He took a step into the room. "But you're crying. You look very upset."

"I—I've had some disturbing news from home."

"But what is it?" He took another step toward her, a look of concern furrowing his brow. "Please tell me." His voice was gentle—quite out of character for him.

She hesitated. "I—I just had a call from my mother. It's my father's illness. He has become very depressed."

"I'm so sorry. Is there anything I can do?"

The note of kindness in Del Toro's voice surprised JoNell. Was he actually capable of showing sympathy for another human being?

"No," she said. "It's a family matter. I hope I can help cheer up my father when I get home."

He glanced toward the bed, saw her packed bags, and frowned. "You are leaving?"

"Yes. We've completed the sales agreement. Ten hours of flying instructions. There's no reason for me to stay any longer. I want to take the earliest commercial flight home that I can get."

Del Toro slumped into a chair, his frown deepening. His green eyes looked dark and troubled. "I had not expected you to be in such a hurry to leave. Is it because I have been such a poor host? You have not been happy in my home? Please forgive me for the bad hospitality I have shown you, señorita. This has been a

67

difficult time for me . . . the presidential election . . . I have been under a great deal of pressure. . . ."

JoNell again noticed the lines of worry and fatigue in his face. For an instant, she almost felt a touch of compassion for him. But her voice was aloof when she replied, "That has nothing to do with it, señor. As I said, I was here to do a job, and that has been completed. Now I must go home."

A strange expression crossed Del Toro's face. There was a strained silence before he spoke again. "Couldn't you delay your trip home for a few days so I can show you more of our city?"

You'd like that, wouldn't you, Del Toro? You suddenly remembered that unfinished matter back on the deserted beach.

"Thank you," she said coldly. "But I have no more time for sightseeing. As I told you, my father's health is growing worse. He has so many business worries in addition to his poor health. I must get back to help him."

"How can you help, señorita?"

"I'm not exactly sure," she admitted. "I was planning to finish college next year, but, of course, now that is out of the question. Instead, somehow, perhaps, I can help save my parents' business. It's the worry about the business that has undermined my father's health so badly."

"His business is not doing well?"

She shook her head. "No, frankly it is not. We were never rich, you understand. But we got by quite nicely. Then the naval base in our area closed last year, and many people moved away. That's when business started dropping off. My father worried a great deal. He tried to keep up a happy front, but he couldn't fool my mother. Finally, the strain was too much for him and he had a heart attack. You couldn't possibly know what it's like to be middle class and lose your business. The airplane you bought from us was a financial boost for a little while, but when that money is gone. . . ." Her voice trailed off as she choked back her tears.

Del Toro frowned again. He arose and began pacing the room, slapping a tightly gripped, folded newspaper against the palm of his left hand. He appeared to be struggling with some kind of inner problem and trying to decide what to do about it.

"I'm going to make you an offer," he said at last.

"An offer?" she asked suspiciously, suddenly very wary of him.

"Let's call it a business proposition that will be of much benefit to both of us." He paused. "You are aware of how busy I have been lately?"

"Yes."

"Here, read this." Del Toro handed JoNell the newspaper he had been holding.

JoNell opened it. "GERALDO GUSTAMENTE WINS ELECTION," said the headlines in Spanish. She recalled that "Gustamente" was one of the names she had seen painted on walls around the city.

Del Toro explained, "It was a bitter fight between Gustamente and the other candidate, Sergio Mendez de Cardova. I backed de Cardova. It was no secret that I gave him all the support I could muster, which is considerable. Unfortunately, it wasn't enough. As you can see, de Cardova lost."

"But what does that have to do with me?" JoNell asked.

"Gustamente considers me his most dangerous political enemy in Peru. He knows that after his inauguration, I will not cease to oppose him. He is an evil man. All he wants is power and wealth for himself. As soon as Gustamente takes office, I will be in a dangerous position."

"I still don't understand."

"You do not know politics here in South America.

Unlike your country, where the will of the people is supreme, in Peru, powerful factions can seize control of the government. It can be very dangerous to be an enemy of the regime in office. Gustamente will surely move to confiscate my business holdings. And he will have the power to do it. In fact," Del Toro said darkly, "my life will be in danger. Gustamente would not hesitate to have political enemies assassinated."

JoNell gasped and a fleeting picture of Del Toro lying in a pool of blood made her shiver. She didn't doubt for one minute that such a possibility existed. Even in the United States, which Del Toro considered so democratic and civilized, assassinations of well known political figures had taken place during her lifetime. And she remembered reading about the assassinations in Cuba when Castro took over. She knew how ruthless power hungry people could be.

"I am making plans now to get out of the country," Del Toro went on.

"But why are you telling me all of this?" JoNell asked a bit impatiently. "Where do I fit in?"

Del Toro gave JoNell a long, steely look. "I know what you think of me," he said bitterly. "But consider carefully what I am going to say. It could be very important for both of us."

He hesitated. The room became almost unbearably tense.

"JoNell, I want you to marry me."

Chapter 5

The newspaper in JoNell's hand dropped to the floor with a whispered crackle. She felt the blood drain from her cheeks.

After the way he had kissed her on the beach, she

had been prepared for any number of tactical maneuvers on his part. But she had never expected this—a proposal of marriage! She knew it had to be a trick. But for what purpose?

"It's strictly a business proposition," he went on without emotion. "When I need to get out of the country, as the husband of an American citizen, I will automatically acquire all the privileges of a citizen of the United States. I can live there and work there as a citizen of your country. I can transfer much of my business and financial holdings there. In return for your doing me this favor, I will buy from your father a large number of airplanes to set up a cargo business in the United States and in other South American countries. Perhaps we can also arrange for your father to have a part in the operation of my air cargo business. So you see, by marrying me, you will save me from Gustamente and you will save your father from financial ruin. It is an important decision for you to make, JoNell."

JoNell felt her heart pounding wildly in her chest. At last, the ruthless, selfish Del Toro was showing his true colors. And for a moment, she had been fooled into believing he felt a genuine concern for her and her family!

Now, it was clear to her, that he had thought of her as an ace up his sleeve from the very beginning. That was why he had suddenly changed his mind and allowed her to give him flying lessons—to keep her here until he saw how the election turned out! Perhaps he had showered her with flowers and his Latin style flattery, thinking that the poor little naive American girl would be an easy conquest. Then she would fall all over herself saying "yes" when he proposed just to get an American wife! When he saw his fatal Del Toro charm wouldn't melt her bitterness toward him, he had been stymied. But now she had given him the key to his problem when she told him of her father's desperate business plight.

"Marry you?" JoNell stormed. "Absolutely not. Never—never—never—!"

Gone were the flowery Latin phrases, the flattery, the macho charm. He spoke coldly and directly. "Don't be too hasty. I need you and you need me. It's strictly business. Surely, you have seen enough transactions in your father's business to know a good deal when you see one. You cannot deny that I am offering you a financial proposition that you can hardly refuse. Think what it will mean to your father : . . to your family. You must not foolishly let your angry feelings for me stand in the way. I am offering to buy a year of your time in exchange for assuring your father's financial future."

"I notice you're talking in English now," she said bitterly. "What happened to all that pretty Spanish you were using when you were trying to seduce me?"

They glared at each other. He looked as if he were on the point of slapping her and barely able to contain himself. She instinctively took a step backward, frightened by the rage in his eyes. He seemed taller, his powerful shoulders even broader.

But he got himself under control. "Bickering at each other will not help matters at this point. Is a year out of your young life such a dreadful price to pay for saving your father's business?"

"A year?"

"Yes. Of course I don't expect you to commit your entire life to me. I just need time to set up my business in the States. I want the marriage to look authentic. I think about a year would do it. Once I'm settled in your country and have my business operating, a divorce can be easily arranged."

"Or an annulment?"

"No, it should be a divorce. The marriage must

appear in all respects to be a valid one. I cannot risk being deported for entering your country fraudulently. It will have to be a divorce."

Her eyes narrowed. A raw, ugly taste crept into her mouth. "Then you expect it to be a real marriage?"

He shook his head. "I told you, it's strictly a business arrangement. But no one must know. Gustamente has spies everywhere. If any of them suspected my plans, my assassination might be undertaken before I have an opportunity to leave Peru. Even my best friends, my family must not know. I trust no one. You must swear to me that you will tell no one, no matter what the circumstances. Otherwise my blood will be on your hands."

JoNell shivered, what had she gotten herself into? A few weeks ago, she had been an average twenty-one-year-old American college girl. She had been looking forward to an uncomplicated life of teaching school and eventually marrying a nice, steady guy and raising a family. And now here she was in the middle of South American political intrigue—a volatile situation she really didn't understand.

She raged inwardly at Del Toro for putting her in this position. Damn him, she thought—he is a demon. What a mockery they would make of the marriage vows. She would be tied for a year to a man who had created in her uncertain and conflicting feelings. It would thrust her into a rich element of Peruvian society that she had only read about in the gossip magazines. She realized with a start that it would transform her from an unknown private citizen into an instant celebrity whose picture was sure to make those same gossip magazines.

No, she thought wildly, I can't do it. Never in a million years.

But at the same time, her conscience nagged her—what about her father? Del Toro was offering her the one way she could really help her family. It would get her parents out of debt, give her father something to live for and save them from financial ruin. Was a year out of her life too high a price to pay to rescue her parents? They would surely do the same and more for her.

Her inner conflict was almost unbearable. All of her instincts for decency and honor screamed at her to say "no" to Del Toro's unholy proposition. But loyalty to her family told her she must make a sacrifice for their sake.

"How do I know you'll keep your end of the bargain and buy those planes from my father?" she demanded.

"As soon as you agree to the marriage, I will call my purchasing agent and order six cargo planes through your father immediately. Then I'll deposit the full purchase price in the bank in your married name. As soon as you become my bride you can authorize payment to your father."

"How do you know I'll keep my end of the agreement?" she asked.

Del Toro grabbed JoNell savagely by the wrist. He pulled her toward him. Again she saw the dangerous fires raging in his eyes. "You wouldn't dare walk out on me," he warned in a growl.

JoNell shivered. She pulled back hard to rescue her wrist and rubbed the red mark where Del Toro's fingers had bitten into her flesh. He was obviously not a man to be toyed with. Whatever her decision, she would have to make it knowing that her suave "suitor" harbored a ruthless side to his nature.

She drew a deep breath, as if about to take a plunge into an icy stream that had dangerous undercurrents. "All—all right," she agreed in a whisper. She regretted the words as soon as she had spoken them. But like her decision to come here in the first place, she really had no choice.

She felt as if the breath had been knocked out of her.

Del Toro's lips moved in a one-sided smile. A look of cool triumph filled his eyes. "I knew you'd see it my way. You won't regret your decision."

"I regret it already," she sighed. "But I'll do anything to help my parents."

Briskly, he said, "To show you I am a man of my word, I will order the planes now." He picked up the telephone. A few moments later, he was speaking in rapid-fire Spanish, telling his purchasing agent to place an immediate order for six expensive cargo planes directly through JoNell's father's business.

Then he turned to her. "There. Satisfied?"

"I suppose so," JoNell murmured.

"Don't look so glum, my dear. You will be the envy of Peru. A number of women will eat their hearts out because you snared me and they didn't. Now, doesn't that make you feel just a little bit smug?"

"Hardly, under the circumstances!"

"But you might as well enjoy your triumph. After all, everyone is going to think it is you who conquered me, not I who conquered you."

"Nobody's conquered anybody," she replied tartly. Then she asked, "How soon do we leave for the States?"

"Not immediately. It will be several weeks before the official inauguration of the new president. I am in no immediate danger from Gustamente until he does take office. Meanwhile, I have many business matters to settle. But we must be married very soon so it will not appear so obvious that I take an American wife and leave the next day for the United States!"

JoNell felt a wave of disappointment. She was homesick for her parents and hoped to see them soon. But she supposed now she would have to live by Del Toro's timetable.

"How about Consuelo?" she asked bitterly. "I

suppose you will keep her in the wings until the year is up and the divorce is taken care of, and then marry her."

He shrugged, giving her a calculating look. "Why do you concern yourself with Consuelo? Are you being a jealous wife, already?"

"Certainly not!" she said furiously. "I just feel sorry for the poor girl, in love with a heartless rat like you!"

His eyes narrowed. She bit her lip, wishing she had not spoken so hastily. He obviously had a fiery temper, and she was pushing it to the breaking point. Somehow, he managed to keep his self-control. He said nothing.

After a moment, she asked, "How soon will the—will we be—married?" She was barely able to get the word past her lips. She felt as if she would choke on it.

"As soon as possible. It will be a civil ceremony. A friend of mine, a judge, can marry us on short notice." He looked at her critically. "First, I would wish to buy you some clothes—"

"I don't want you to buy me anything!" she flared.

His green eyes smoldered. "Nevertheless, we will shop for a new wardrobe for you tomorrow. You must not forget for one minute that you will be the wife of Jorge Del Toro, and so you must dress and look the part at all times."

"Well, since you have hired me, in a manner of speaking, I suppose I must do as you say." She turned away, rubbing her left wrist with her right hand. "I must break the news to my parents, somehow," she said, talking half to herself. "I don't know exactly how to do it. I just finished telling my mother that I was catching the next plane home. . . ."

"I will leave that up to you. I am sure you will handle the matter in the way that you think best. Just remember that you are sworn to secrecy. Even your parents must not know the real reason for the marriage."

"You don't think I'd tell them, do you?" she raged, swinging back to face him with a look of fury. "If my father guessed for even a moment that you are 'buying' me this way, it would surely kill him!"

"Very well, just so we understand each other."

"Just so we understand this is a business arrangement," she reminded him. "I want your handshake on that."

She held out her hand to him.

He touched her fingers, giving her an intense look. Suddenly, without warning, his hand closed around hers. He jerked her up against him, and kissed her furiously.

"A kiss is much more binding than a handshake," he said in Spanish, and stalked out of the room.

JoNell sank into a chair, her legs turned to rubber, her mouth bruised and stinging. Tears of impotent rage filled her eyes.

By the next morning, all of Del Toro's household vibrated with the news of the coming marriage. JoNell assumed he had called the servants together and made the announcement last night that the household would soon have a new mistress. The maid giggled and shot JoNell a meaningful glance, rolling her eyes as she opened the drapes to let in the morning sunlight.

When Miguel brought her breakfast tray, his round face was beaming like a new moon. "Señorita, I am so happy, I prayed to my favorite saint that love would come to you and the señor. My prayers were answered. Now I pray for your happiness and for many, many children that you will have."

JoNell blushed furiously. She managed to mumble an appropriate answer, wishing she could pull the covers over her head and hide. She was getting her first taste of how miserable this deception was going to make her feel.

Miguel bustled around, arranging fresh flowers on

her breakfast tray. "The señor asked me to tell you that he wishes to take you to the stores to buy you many new dresses after you have eaten breakfast."

"Very well," JoNell muttered. How she despised Del Toro! He was giving her orders as if he owned her—and why not? He was paying a handsome price for her. She supposed at least she could salvage a little pride by reminding herself that she had not come cheap. The amount he was paying for those six large cargo planes was staggering. Of course, he wasn't just giving the money away. The cargo planes would become part of his business empire.

"The first thing I'd better do," JoNell mused after Miguel had left the room, "is call my mother."

How was she going to break the news to her family? She rehearsed several speeches. She practiced sounding excited and happy. It wasn't easy. Not when she was on the ragged edge of tears.

"I suppose," she thought, "I'll start by telling mother that we're engaged. I'll say it was a whirlwind romance. I'll gradually lead up to the fact that we'll be married here in Peru in a matter of days."

Then she reminded herself that only yesterday she had told her mother that she was catching the earliest possible flight home. She hadn't mentioned a word about a romance with Del Toro.

"This is going to take some tall explaining," she mused. "Okay, this is what I'll tell her: I'll say that Del Toro has been pursuing me ever since I got here. I won't exactly be lying about *that*," she thought grimly. "I can say we had a lovers' quarrel, and I told him I was going home. But last night we made up and Del Toro popped the question. He asked me to marry him and I accepted. I can tell mother to decide the best way to break the news to Daddy so it won't be too much of a shock or upset him."

She felt dreadful, having to make up the lie. She'd

78

never lied to her parents about anything important before in her life. She knew her mother would be crushed, not being able to attend her daughter's wedding. She knew how her parents had dreamed about the day their little girl would walk down the aisle on her daddy's arm.

"I'll tell them we're moving to the States as soon as Jorge settles his business arrangements. That will make mother feel somewhat better."

She drew a deep breath and reached for the telephone.

An hour later, she was beside Del Toro in the Rolls Royce. Miguel was driving them to a shopping district of high fashion stores.

JoNell was acutely aware of Del Toro's broad shoulder touching hers, and the masculine scent of his shaving lotion. His powerfully built athletic body seemed to fill the car seat as it had the airplane cockpit. He was wearing a dark suit tailored of expensive fabric, a very pale lavender shirt with a matching, darker lavender tie. A diamond tie tack sparkled when he moved. In his lapel was a white carnation.

"Have you called your mother?" he asked.

"Yes. I called her this morning," JoNell replied frostily. "She cried."

"I am sorry. But then all mothers cry when their daughters announce that they are betrothed."

"If she knew the truth about this wedding, she'd have good reason to cry," JoNell said bitterly. "By the way, she didn't say anything about the cargo planes."

"My purchasing agent will contact your father today. It was late yesterday that I gave the order, and there is paper work involved in a purchase this large."

The dress shops had the most elegant sales rooms JoNell had ever seen. Chandeliers gleamed in the soft, indirect lighting. Feet sank deep in plush carpeting. In the ambience of hushed, quiet dignity there was heard only the rustle of garments being modeled and the murmur of the shop owner. It was the rarified atmosphere of haute couture familiar only to the very rich. As much as she resented Del Toro's dragging her here, JoNell couldn't help but feel like a princess (albeit a reluctant one!) as the models paraded exquisite design creations for her approval.

But it was Del Toro who studied the garments with a critical eye and made the decisions. A flick of his finger or a slight disapproving shake of his head signaled the acceptance or rejection of a frock. His imperial attitude added fuel to JoNell's fury. She felt like a child being outfitted by an autocratic parent.

Even so, she had to grudgingly admit that Del Toro had impeccable taste. Every gown he chose flattered her as if the designer had planned that of all the women in the world, the lines of his creation were made to flow around her body alone.

The fashion coordinator snapped her wrist disdainfully to shoo away a model when Del Toro frowned at a creation. When he saw a dress he liked, JoNell was whisked into a dressing room where three seamstresses pinned and marked how the garment was to be altered to fit her slender form. Not once did Del Toro ask about price.

He wasn't satisfied until JoNell had a complete wardrobe ranging from sportswear to dinner gowns. Much to her agonizing embarrassment, the wardrobe included filmy negligees and wispy undergarments.

She was relieved when the shopping expedition came to an end and she was settled in the back of the Rolls Royce, surrounded by boxes filled with garments that bore such labels as Givenchy, Christian Dior, Gucci, Saint Laurent and Fontana.

She supposed that Del Toro felt the purchases were necessary. He could hardly go around Lima with a wife dressed in jump suits and sneakers! But the end result was to make her feel like a kept woman. His highhanded method of dragging her down here and choosing the clothes for her robbed her of another shred of self-respect. Maybe she would have been more at home with a monkey wrench and a spark plug than choosing between a gown by Givenchy or Saint Laurent, but she didn't need to have Del Toro making her acutely aware of that fact.

He did not get into the car with her. Instead, he closed her door, then leaned down, thrusting his head through the opened window. "Miguel will take you home. I will take a taxi. I have some more matters to attend to."

On the drive home, in spite of her anger at Del Toro, she felt a sense of anticipation. She could spend the rest of the day sampling the delicious feel of dresses by the world's foremost designers. She could try them on to her heart's content. Despite the unpleasantness of the situation, she reasoned she might as well let herself enjoy the new wardrobe. What woman wouldn't feel some measure of excitement at having this kind of wardrobe in her closet?

When she entered her room, she found another huge basket of roses with the usual flowery note. "To express my deep love and admiration for my most beautiful bride-to-be." JoNell shook her head in disgust, crumpled the note and flung it into a wastebasket. You'd think, she reasoned, that since Del Toro had shown his true colors and admitted his interest in her was purely a selfish, business one, to save his own hide from Gustamente, that he would drop the phony Latin flattery. But she supposed, the macho image was so ingrained in him, he just had to keep going through the motions.

About five o'clock, JoNell was having the customary Peruvian afternoon snack, the lunch, consisting of tea, a hard roll and pastry, when a familiar voice from the doorway startled her. "Did you talk with your father today?"

"You have a nasty habit of sneaking up on people!" JoNell said shortly, turning to glare at Del Toro.

"Perhaps I should wear a bell around my neck, my love?"

"Don't be sarcastic, and I wish you'd stop calling me 'my love' in private. I don't like it."

"I am only practicing so I will not forget when we are in public. Remember, we must convince all of Peru that we are a loving couple."

She chose to ignore his remark. "Yes, I did talk with my father—or rather with my Uncle Edgar to be specific. He was at the airport office when I called. He confirmed that they have received the order for the cargo planes. He says my father is overjoyed. My Uncle Edgar also sends his congratulations and blessing. Says he must have misjudged you completely." She laughed bitterly. "Of course I didn't tell him that he had judged you quite correctly."

Del Toro flushed angrily. "Can't you think of our arrangement as mutually beneficial? I'm helping you, and you're helping me. It would make things so much more pleasant between us."

But JoNell refused to be swayed by Del Toro's suave exterior. "There's absolutely no reason to pretend to be nice to each other," she said dryly. "We have a business arrangement, that's all. Let's keep it impersonal."

Suddenly, Del Toro appeared to be distracted by something. The room fell silent as he listened, a slight frown touching his brow.

"What is it?" JoNell asked.

He raised a hand to silence her. JoNell heard a faint tinkling. Her gaze swung to her dressing table and became horrified when she saw the bottles of cologne vibrating. Next she was aware of a window rattling softly. The light fixture above her swung a fraction.

She felt something ominous in the atomosphere. "What is it?" she gasped with sudden fright.

"It is an earthquake tremor."

"Oh!" JoNell cried. Fear blotted out her dislike for Del Toro. Without thinking about it, she rushed to the nearest source of security—Del Toro's arms.

He held her tightly, gazing down with an expression of mocking amusement. "Is this how we keep our arrangement 'impersonal'? Not too bad!"

JoNell was so startled and disconcerted by her fear of the earthquake tremor that she didn't pull away, and the next thing she realized, his lips crushed down on hers. For a giddy instant, she felt that same unwanted emotional response she had felt that day on the deserted beach, a physical awakening of her body, pressing harder against his, a fire springing to life deep inside her, threatening to turn into raging desire.

But instantly, she came to her senses and jerked back from him. "That's not part of our deal!" she flared.

"You came to me," he reminded her.

"The earthquake frightened me, and you took advantage of it. You don't have any scruples at all where a woman is concerned, do you?"

JoNell felt rage in Del Toro's stare as he raked his eyes over her. For a moment the air in the room fairly sizzled with the clash of their emotions. But gradually, the anger in Del Toro's eyes drained away and logic took its place. Or was it cool calculation, as he weighed his fury against her importance to his safety? She thought that he had been near the point of telling her to forget their business deal and sending her packing on the first commercial flight home—but then had thought better of it.

He rammed his hand into the pocket of his snug-fitting trousers. In spite of herself, JoNell couldn't help but notice, with an unwanted tingle, how smoothly the rich brown fabric hugged the powerful muscles of his thighs.

"Here!" Del Toro thrust his hand angrily at her. He was holding a small, velvet covered box.

"What is it?"

"Open it and find out."

She lifted the cover. Her breath caught in her throat. Nestled in a black velvet cushion was an enormous solitary diamond in a simple gold ring setting. The diamond flashed blue-white fire with each movement of the box.

"It's your engagement ring," Del Toro said. "Why don't you put it on? Or better yet, let me put it on your finger."

JoNell got her breath back. She held the box out to him. "I can't accept this," she gasped. "You can't be serious."

"Of course I am serious. One doesn't buy a diamond like this for a joke! And you will accept it. You are the fiancée of Jorge Del Toro, and you will wear an appropriate ring."

Again she felt the impotent rage of being backed into an emotional corner. "I will not be beholden to you," she insisted, raising her chin. "I want it clearly understood that the day the marriage is ended, the ring goes back to you."

"You're a stubborn little fool!" Del Toro stormed. "Do you know how many women would jump at the chance to marry Jorge Del Toro even for one year? But you find excuses to riddle our marriage with hatred. Can't you relax and enjoy yourself once in a while? A year is a long time to hate someone you're going to have to live with."

JoNell glared at him. "I am different from all those other women in one important respect."

"And what is that?"

"You weren't able to mesmerize me with your so-called Latin flattery and charm the way you were the others. I know you for what you are!"

Dark green eyes clashed with large brown ones. Then the dark green eyes began to crinkle around the corners, and Del Toro threw back his head and laughed heartily.

"You are insufferable!" JoNell cried.

"So insufferable that you refuse to marry me—so insufferable that you would let your father lose his business rather than spend a year as my wife?"

JoNell's eyes filled with angry tears. "I knew you were totally without scruples, señor," she said in measured tones. "But I had no idea you were also sadistic. Does it amuse you to taunt me?"

"Not so much as it pleases me to tell you when and where our wedding will take place."

JoNell gulped a chunk of air that felt sharp and pointed. She steeled herself to hear details which she had not wanted to think about. Until now, the prospect of actually going through the wedding ceremony with Jorge Del Toro had been a specter floating in the hazy future. But confronting the specific details of the wedding would rob her ethereal phantom of its elusive quality and plunge her into harsh reality.

"Can't it wait?" she resisted sullenly.

"No. We must have the wedding soon, within a matter of days. I must start immediately to make arrangements to transfer my business to the United States. I need my citizenship rights as your husband now. I cannot wait until Gustamente takes office. That would be too late."

JoNell wiped her moist brow. An invisible band

tightened around her throat. "All right," she murmured in a resigned voice. "Let's hear it."

From that moment, JoNell's life played like a slow motion movie.

In her mind, Del Toro's words stretched out interminably as he described the simple civil ceremony they would have. She felt herself in a long, dark room, viewing her movements on a small movie screen. From this vantage point, she saw herself choose a lemon-white suit for what was, for her, a wedding in her mind only. She didn't realize that her detachment from the whole situation was a mental trick to preserve emotionally her unmarried state. On paper and in name, she would be Mrs. Jorge Del Toro. But in body and spirit, she fiercely clung to her identity as JoNell Carpenter, unmarried and still entitled, one day, to a full white wedding with a long bridal gown. Technically, she would one day become a divorcée. But her mind would refuse to relinquish her self-image as a never married, single girl.

In her thoughts, JoNell remained in her bedroom for the next forty-eight hours, never stepping outside to accompany Del Toro to register their marriage, not riding in the back of his Rolls Royce to the chambers of a political friend of Del Toro's, a judge, who married them.

There was a dream-like quality to the sequence of events, a defensive state of mind that insulated her from unpleasant reality.

The cold shock of reality washed over her only when she looked down at the third finger of her left hand, and there, next to the costly diamond engagement ring Del Toro had given her, nestled a diamond encrusted wedding band! She stared at the rings. They seemed to weigh her hand down.

Then they were in the limousine. "We will have dinner out tonight," Del Toro said, "to celebrate."

She looked at the tall, elegantly dressed man beside

her. A bewildered voice inside her said, this man, this stranger, *is your husband*. She closed her eyes against hot tears that threatened to spill over. "Celebrate what?" she asked dully. "The closing of a business deal?"

Del Toro chose not to reply. He appeared to be in an expansive mood. He gave an order to Miguel in Spanish. The limousine whisked them to one of Lima's elegant dinner clubs. "We must start the evening with a toast," Del Toro exclaimed, and instructed the waiter to bring them two Pisco Sours. "In Peru, everyone drinks Pisco Sours," he smiled to JoNell.

When the drinks arrived, Del Toro touched his glass to hers. "To a happy and pleasant relationship for the next year."

"To a business relationship," she corrected bitterly.

The drink was delicious and deceptively mild. "What's in it?" she asked.

"Pisco is a raw brandy made from grapes and sugar," he explained. "Lemon juice, sugar and a beaten egg white are added to the Pisco and mixed in a shaker with ice."

"It's very good. I think I'd like another."

"Very well, but I should warn you that a Pisco Sour is like a time bomb that may go off later in the evening."

She shrugged away his warning. If the drink numbed her mind, so much the better. It might make this sad evening more bearable.

They had a second round of drinks while Del Toro poured over the menu, then ordered dinner with a bottle of vintage French champagne.

JoNell thought that she could buy a new carburetor for her airplane back home for what the champagne was no doubt costing Del Toro. "I wish you wouldn't order such a large dinner for me," she protested. "I'm not hungry." Her tongue felt slightly thick.

"You should eat," Del Toro said. "Two Pisco Sours

on an empty stomach. . . ." He shook his head. "And I venture to say you are not accustomed to alcoholic drinks."

"We always keep a bottle of wine in the house for special occasions," she said recklessly.

That brought a chuckle from him, but she couldn't see what was so funny. She realized she was having some problem focusing her eyes. Her tongue was growing even thicker and more difficult to manage.

Presently, a retinue of waiters swooped down on their table with numerous trays. A salad was tossed before her. Flaming dishes were ignited. A champagne cork popped. Strolling musicians gathered around their table and serenaded them.

JoNell felt embarrassingly conspicuous. She became aware that people at other tables were looking their way, whispering, nodding and smiling at them. She tried to hide behind her napkin. "People are staring at us!" she whispered angrily.

"Of course," he smiled. "You are the bride of Jorge Del Toro. You are now the toast of Peru."

"I don't want to be th' thoast of—I mean, th' toast of anything!" she said furiously.

"Eat your dinner. You're getting tipsy."

"Am not!" she flared, raising her chin. But she only poked at her food.

The events of the evening grew hazy. Eventually she was aware that dinner had ended. Del Toro had enjoyed his food with gusto and consumed most of the champagne. When he escorted her from the table, he kept a firm hand under her arm. As much as she hated herself for having to do so, she was obliged to lean against him for support. "I warned you about two Pisco Sours on an empty stomach," he grinned.

She shot him a dirty look, but said nothing, afraid to trust her tongue at this point.

"Now be prepared," he said. "When we go out to the

car, there will be reporters and photographers. They are not allowed in the dinner club."

In answer to her look of mingled distress and anger, he confessed, "Yes, I notified the press. It is important for all of Peru to know about this wedding. I told you, there can be nothing secret about it. We must convince everyone that the marriage is real."

Then they were outside. Photographic electronic flashes blazed in her eyes. Reporters gathered around them. JoNell was stunned to see a mobile television unit on the scene. Del Toro held up his hand and made a brief statement. "My bride, señora JoNell Del Toro Carpenter," he introduced, following the Peruvian custom of including her maiden name as a second last name. "Señora Del Toro came to this country from the United States to give me flying lessons. We fell in love at first sight and were married tonight by my friend, Judge de la Cuestra. We will be at my home in Lima for the present time and, in a few weeks, will take a delayed honeymoon trip to the United States."

JoNell was impressed by Del Toro's suave composure. He towered over the reporters and photographers, a commanding presence exhibiting supreme self-confidence and control of the situation. As for herself, she wanted to sink out of sight through a hole in the ground. She was grateful that a Peruvian wife would be expected to be silent and let her husband do the talking.

There was the drive home, of which JoNell remembered very little, and the stairs to navigate when again she was forced to accept Del Toro's amused assistance. She vowed that never again would she have one of the insidious Pisco Sours on an empty stomach!

At last she was in the safety of her room. She slipped out of her lemon-white wedding suit and into one of the filmy nightgowns that were now part of her costly wardrobe. She switched off the light, and started walking unsteadily toward her bed, when suddenly a shaft of light cut across the floor. She spun around. Outlined in the doorway was the broad-shouldered silhouette of Jorge Del Toro.

"What do you want?" she demanded.

"I just came to see if you were safely in bed. You were not in a very steady condition coming up the stairs."

"I'm perfectly all right," she lied. Actually, her head was spinning and her thought processes were still somewhat befuddled.

Then she realized that he was continuing to stand there, staring at her. She became aware of the revealing nature of her diaphanous gown. She was standing before a ceiling-to-floor window with bright moonlight behind her, outlining every inch of her body. She snatched a negligee from a nearby chair, holding it against her bosom. "Please go," she said in an unsteady voice.

But, instead, he moved toward her. She shrank back against the window. Del Toro towered over her. In the moonlight, she could see his eyes ablaze with desire as they drank in the sight of her figure.

She began shivering. It was the deserted beach all over again. But this time she saw a raw hunger in his face beyond any power to control.

"Please—" she whimpered.

She saw a struggle in his eyes. Then, with a broken cry, he seized her and buried his face against her throat. She heard him murmur her name in broken phrases.

"Oh, no—no—" she begged, trying with all her strength to push him away.

But his arms had become bands of steel that swept her up and carried her to the bed.

She felt his scorching kisses on her face, the hollow of her throat, on her breasts. Dimly, she heard her gown tear, heard the stifled, choked sounds of her protests and pleading, and the rough sound of his voice murmuring her name.

One moment he was tender, the next demanding, but at no time could she escape his towering strength. He held her prisoner, but he did not have to resort entirely to force. Instead, he kissed and caressed her until slowly a responsive fire awakened in her. She despised him for this power he had over her, and she hated herself with equal rancor for feeling the desire that was making her heart pound and her body quiver.

What a wicked power Del Toro had over her—and he had known it since that first kiss on the beach. He had agreed to a marriage in name only, knowing full well that he could awaken these fires in her when he wished. They were both being consumed by passion—but it was passion without love. She did not love Jorge Del Toro, and she knew he certainly did not love her. He had made it quite clear that she was his passport into the United States, nothing more.

Still, those thoughts were swept away by this wild need that now molded them together. The present excitement was all that mattered. She gave herself willingly, freely and wholly. She throbbed at his every touch, his every movement. He led her to heights of fulfillment beyond anything she had dreamed possible. He was a skillful lover who left no avenue of passion untouched.

But, inevitably, the insanity abated. The desires satisfied, cooled. Cold and unpleasant reality took the place of rapture.

Dawn was creeping through the windows when Del Toro arose to leave her. She saw his face shadowed by a changing pattern of emotions.

"I suppose you think this makes me feel differently," she choked. "It does—it makes me hate you even more, for doing this to me, knowing that what I felt was only physical, that I did not . . . do not love you. Hate . . . only hate—"

His eyes were solemn, then angry. He turned without a word and stalked from the room.

She turned to the wall and wept in her loneliness and heartache. A loveless marriage. What a sad, forlorn phrase that was. . . .

Chapter 6

JoNell rubbed her fingers gingerly over the soft velvet of her gold gown with its exquisite lace inset bodice. She studied her mirror reflection with a feeling of awe and fright. Tonight, Del Toro was giving a party to introduce her to Peruvian society. His important friends were, at this moment, approaching the house in their limousines. And what would they see when they were greeted by the new hostess of the Del Toro mansion? A young woman in an exquisite gown complemented by a jade necklace, a sophisticated blond upswept hair style, manicured fingernails and professionally applied makeup—all the product of an entire afternoon in one of Lima's more expensive beauty salons.

The guests would critically scrutinize the outer trappings of the new señora Jorge Del Toro, who came from a middle-class American family. While she was sure they would notice and evaluate her every move, she wondered whether they would also notice the bleak look in her frightened brown eyes and the quivering of her lips as she tried to maintain her composure.

"Might as well get it over with," JoNell thought resignedly.

A week had passed since she became Del Toro's bride. She had seen little of her husband this week. He had been totally occupied with his business. He was gone when she awoke in the mornings, and often came in late at night after she was in bed; and some nights he didn't come home at all, leaving word that he had to be away overnight on business. He had not tried to invade her bedroom since their wedding night, but she felt it was only a matter of time before he visited her bed again. She dreaded that moment. Passion without love was a travesty of the sacred meaning of marriage. Yet, she knew her own weakness where his kisses were concerned. He would rekindle the fires and she would respond physically. But the needs of the flesh were not the needs of the heart. Theirs was a union without soul, without meaning, without love. She would cry again for the young dream of love that had been so cruelly taken from her, and she would hate him for doing this to her.

She had tried not to think about it this past week. She had occupied herself with tennis and swimming at the ultra posh country club where Del Toro had a membership. Once, she'd had Miguel drive her to the airport, and she had taken Del Toro's plane up for a brief flight by herself. Alone, in the clouds, she had experienced a few moments of peace and freedom. She'd had a rash impulse to turn the plane in the direction of the United States and flee this trap she'd fallen into. But sanity forced her to turn, instead, back to the airport and she had reluctantly landed.

Now, she moved out of her room to the hallway, gathering her courage before descending the stairs.

"Good evening, señora Del Toro," a masculine voice murmured at her elbow.

She swung around, raising her chin as intense green eyes raked over her. "Good evening, señor Del Toro," she replied coldly.

"You must remember to call me Jorge, my dear," he reminded her. "I expect you to be convincing in public."

"Am I dressed properly? Am I walking correctly? Do I please you?" she asked sardonically.

"Almost as much as on our wedding night," he replied huskily.

She felt her cheeks burn scarlet. Quickly, she changed the subject, although something inside her tingled at the thought of Del Toro's body so dangerously near hers.

"Will Consuelo be here tonight?"

"Of course. She is from one of the leading families in Peru. How would it look if I excluded her?"

JoNell bit her bottom lip, but said no more.

Naturally, Del Toro would want Consuelo here. She was the woman he loved, after all.

JoNell walked down the winding stairway on Del Toro's arm to the main ballroom where a flurry of activity was taking place. Waiters in dinner jackets bustled with last minute preparations. Musicians wearing gold lamé vests took instruments from well-polished cases and thumbed through sheets of musical arrangements. A table across one side of the huge room had a large, ornate golden crown suspended in midair above it. The table was weighed down with fruits, appetizers and hors d'oeuvres.

"Do you like it?" Del Toro asked, with a broad sweep of his arm.

"A little on the ostentatious side," JoNell said flatly. Then she regretted her lukewarm response. Del Toro's expression dimmed. Why should she care that the bright sparkle in his deep green eyes had turned cold, she wondered?

"Is it so important to impress your friends? Do you really care so much what society thinks?"

"It is vital to me what they think."

She remembered that he had made it quite clear how dangerous his political enemies were.

"But surely you can't have any enemies among your friends? This is a party, not a political rally."

"I can trust no one." He smiled indulgently. "You do not understand these political matters. This party is part of the plan to convince all of Lima that ours is a real marriage, and not just a matter of expediency. This is extremely important to me, as I have explained."

"I still wish you hadn't invited Consuelo."

"Why not? Do you feel she's a threat to you?"

JoNell flushed angrily. "Of course not. I know she's in love with you, and you with her—as much as you are capable of feeling love. It means nothing to me. I just think it doesn't look right. Everyone expected you to marry her. Instead, you married me. And now you invite her to this party, as if to flaunt your new bride in her face. Do you really think that's very considerate?"

JoNell knew that her concern was not entirely for the feelings of Consuelo Garcia. That demure young woman had proven she was quite capable of looking out for herself. It was the prospect of another verbal attack by Consuelo that disturbed JoNell.

But there was no more time for discussion; the guests were arriving. JoNell moved beside Del Toro to receive the guests.

In spite of being forewarned, JoNell was overwhelmed by the opulence of the occasion. Her head began spinning as Del Toro murmured introductions. She found herself face to face with governors, movie stars, artists, and industrialists. Even the American ambassador was present.

JoNell tried to guess at the number of extra pounds of jewelry the women were transporting on their well-costumed bodies. She mentally undressed all the guests and placed their clothing and jewelry on one side of an imaginary scale and the naked people on the other side of the scale. The clothes and jewelry won out. The idea was so ludicrous that JoNell almost giggled aloud. She realized with a start that hysteria was bubbling up in her, and her mental game had been a form of defense against having to mingle with people who she felt sure must hold her in contempt because of her middle-class background.

The giggle died a sudden death when JoNell's eyes fell on pale skin against ink black hair. Consuelo had entered the room.

"Let's dance," JoNell said breathlessly to Del Toro. At that moment, she preferred the arms of the man who had bribed her into a loveless marriage rather than the deadly sting of Consuelo's blazing stare.

"At your service, my love," he smiled. "We really should greet the rest of the guests, but no one will fault me for that oversight when they see why I have chosen to neglect them." He signaled to the orchestra leader.

The soft strains of a pachanga carried JoNell and Del Toro rhythmically across the floor. She was not surprised to find Del Toro a skillful dancer. And, because of her Cuban friends back home, she was familiar with most of the Latin dances. She moved lightly in Del Toro's strong arms.

Then she realized to her horror that she and Del Toro were the only couple dancing! A hundred eyes were following her every movement.

When the dance ended, JoNell tried to pull herself loose from Del Toro's arms. But he grabbed her wrist and pulled her close again as the strains of a marinera filled the room. This time other couples joined them. Del Toro held JoNell tightly. His hard, masculine body threatened her even through her heavy velvet gown.

He was carrying off the act beautifully, looking for all the world like a proud man guarding his most prized possession. He kept JoNell on the floor through the entire set, gracefully leading her through a tango, a samba and a rumba. His eyes bore into hers, sending cold shivers down her spine. She tried to look away, but when she did, she encountered Consuelo's searing stare.

When the music finally paused for an intermission, Del Toro's friends crowded around them both, and JoNell found herself being introduced to the guests who had not reached the receiving line when the dance began.

She smiled politely and hoped she said all the right things. But inside, she felt bitterly alone and out of place.

She greeted a guest and her gaze encountered a pair of deep, black eyes set in a thin, dark face.

"Good evening, señora. My name is Rafael Garcia. My prayers and good wishes go to bless your marriage," he murmured in a perfunctory manner. But his intense black eyes lingered on her face.

"Thank you," she said matter-of-factly.

She expected the slender young man to wander off after the obligatory greeting, but he remained. "You look beautiful, señora. We do not see many blondes in Peru. It is refreshing to behold such a stunning, light-haired señora."

"Thank you," she said, a trifle embarrassed. She knew Latin men loved to toss around the flowery phrases, but she was still uneasy when she was the object of their flattery.

"That dress was just made for you. Do you have any idea how it enhances your already gorgeous figure?"

"Please," JoNell protested. "I—I don't know what to say."

"But you need not say anything. Anyone as beautiful as you need do nothing but look lovely."

"Thank you," JoNell faltered again. She felt a

growing warmth edging up her cheeks. Unlike Latin women, she was not versed in all the proper responses for this kind of attention.

"Now, if you will excuse me," she mumbled demurely, her eyes cast downward. She headed toward one of the downstairs bathrooms that had been designated for the women, when she encountered something that made her stop dead in her tracks. Standing squarely in her path was Consuelo! JoNell was much too flustered to take on her arch rival in a bitter verbal battle. She turned on her heels and detoured to a balcony overlooking the inner courtyard.

A gentle breeze caressed her warm cheeks and soothed her tormented feelings. She stood with her hands on the cool marble railing, breathing deeply, her eyes half-closed. She sighed audibly.

"What is the matter, señora?" asked a masculine voice from behind her.

JoNell turned. Silhouetted against the light coming through the French doors stood the man who had moments before been flattering her so lavishly.

"Oh, you startled me," JoNell exclaimed.

"I am very sorry, señora," he said earnestly. He took a step toward her. "You, of all people, I do not want to frighten."

"I wasn't scared. I just didn't expect you, that's all."

"I hope you don't mind that I followed you," he said, moving to her side.

"You followed me? Why?"

"I thought it was obvious, señora."

"Well, I'm afraid it isn't," she said uneasily.

"Señora, you cannot know what it does to me when I look at you."

"Señor. . . ."

"Please call me Rafael. It would give my poor heart such pleasure to hear you call me by my first name."

"But, señor, we have just met. I'm not sure it's proper."

"When a man feels about a woman the way I feel about you, that makes it proper."

"Señor, please. I am a married woman."

"Only because I met you too late," he said sadly.

"How can you say such things? You don't know a thing about me."

"I know all I need to know. You are beautiful . . . bewitching . . . breathtaking—"

"Señor!" she protested again. "Please! You say too much!"

"There is no way I could say too much to one who is so captivating."

"My husband may come looking for me. If he overhears you. . . ."

"Would you really mind?" he asked.

"Of course."

"I think you say that because you think you must. But you mustn't let Jorge Del Toro bully you into staying in a marriage that does not make you happy."

JoNell stared at him. Could this man, a total stranger, read the unhappiness in her eyes? Was it that obvious?

"Del Toro—Jorge—has not bullied me into anything," she lied.

"You cannot be happy with him," he said.

"How can you know anything about what makes me happy?"

"Because I know Del Toro. I have known him all his life. And now that I have seen you, I know you too."

"No, you don't."

"Forgive me, señora, but I do. Deny that you are a gentle woman, compassionate, warm and vulnerable."

Unnerved by this display of familiarity, JoNell was at a loss to know how to answer him.

He went on, "Deny that your marriage to Del Toro does not cause you deep trouble. I saw it in your face and eyes when you were dancing with him. I watched you closely."

"You have no right—"

"I have every right. My attraction to you gives me that right."

"Señor—"

"Rafael."

"Señor," she repeated emphatically, "you overstep the bounds of propriety. I know that Latin men love to flatter women, but you have gone much too far. Save your compliments for a señorita who is not married. Why do you waste them on me, a married woman?"

"Because I have never known any woman who set my heart on fire the way you do. Your marriage does not stand in the way of my feelings. You do not have to stay married if you are unhappy. Even in Peru, it is possible to get a divorce, and according to the newspapers it was a civil ceremony, so the church would not stand in the way."

"You must be insane," JoNell said.

"Yes, señora, I am insane. I have been driven insane by my torment because you are married to another man."

JoNell realized she could have ended the conversation by simply walking away. But there was something quite appealing about the ardent young man. His flattery was one of the most elaborate lines she had ever heard, even for a Latin. But behind the compliments, she sensed a certain tension which was absent in the patter of most Latin men when they were trying to woo a señorita. There was a boyish honesty about Rafael, almost as if he truly meant what he said. Yet, something was amiss. He was overly controlled in his manner, as if walking a tightrope with careful maneuvers. The contrast between what appeared to be genuine honesty and what she sensed to be an inner disturbance was a mystery that intrigued her, so she remained and listened.

"Rafael—" the name came easily, now that she had seen his naive quality, "—perhaps you do find me attractive. I guess that's not so hard for me to believe. Just the fact that I have blond hair makes me stand out. I've already realized that in the short time I've been here. But—" she searched for the right words, not wanting to hurt the sensitive young man.

"Yes?" he asked eagerly.

"Uh—don't you think you're overdoing it a bit? Peruvian women may be used to hearing such exaggerated flattery. But to an American it sounds a little—unbelievable," was the most polite word she could think of.

"But it comes from my heart," Rafael protested.

"Señor, I must ask you to excuse me," JoNell said, turning to leave.

"No, don't go," he pleaded. "I have so much more to say."

"You've already said more than I cared to hear," she said as kindly as she knew how.

"Wait. When can I see you again?" he asked.

"It is out of the question, señor. Good night."

As she moved past him, Rafael put out his arm and caught JoNell around the waist. He pulled her to him slowly, gently. "The bride cannot deny me one kiss," he said softly. "Surely I am entitled to that."

JoNell was struck by the difference between this man and the man she had been forced by circumstances to marry. Rafael was a considerate, sensitive man who approached her as one would reach out to a prized flower. His touch was soft and caring. Del Toro, on the other hand, was a self-centered egotist who wrested what he wanted from life by force, regardless of the damage it might cause others.

"Regretfully, you are not," she responded, truly sorry that she could not find it in herself to grant him that which he so desperately sought.

She pulled herself free of his grasp and fled into the ballroom, thankful to be among the very people she had just recently shunned.

"Good evening . . . señora," said a demure, feminine voice, with an unpleasant emphasis on the word señora.

JoNell's vision cleared from the fog she had surrounded herself with as a protective veil. The image of large black eyes, creamy pale skin, and a halo of black hair came into focus. JoNell groaned inwardly.

"I see you did not take my advice," said Consuelo Garcia frostily. "You'll be sorry. I know what I'm talking about when it comes to Jorge Del Toro."

"Maybe you don't know him as well as you think you do," JoNell bristled. In spite of feeling sorry for Consuelo, JoNell didn't appreciate the way the other woman had cast slurs on her background during their previous encounter. Consuelo's thinly veiled insults had left her with a certain amount of defensive hostility.

"I know Jorge well enough to be certain of one thing," Consuelo said smugly. "He does not love you. He loves me. And when he tires of you, he will cast you aside like so much used property."

JoNell had no answer for that, for in her heart she knew Consuelo spoke the truth.

"Jorge and I grew up side by side, both from the same kind of families, both with the same background. How long have you known him? What do you have in common with him?"

JoNell saw Consuelo twist slender fingers tightly around the stem of the goblet she was holding. The air had grown oppressive. JoNell felt as if a tight corset were squeezing the breath out of her.

"Hello, señor Hernandez," Consuelo said sweetly to a tall man who walked by. But her smile faded as señor Hernandez melted into the crowd, and her eyes grew cold again.

"You're nothing but a gold digger," Consuelo went on. "When you look at Del Toro, you have dollar signs in your eyes."

"How dare you!" JoNell gasped.

"I dare because Jorge belongs to me. You may have him now, señora, but I assure you it will be only a temporary condition. You have nothing that could have forced Jorge to marry you except for one thing—Jorge married you for your United States citizenship."

JoNell's breath caught in her throat. An icy hand squeezed her stomach. How could Consuelo possibly know about her business arrangement with Del Toro? Her startled mind felt like a computer gone berserk with all its lights flashing and cards shooting out wildly in all directions. This was the one thing Del Toro feared. Under no circumstances, he had warned JoNell, was she to reveal their secret—not even to her family.

And yet Consuelo knew. Or made a lucky guess.

There was another explanation, JoNell realized. Del Toro might have taken Consuelo into his confidence. He loved this woman and he wanted her to know his marriage was only temporary. After all, she was the one person he could trust. Her love for him would guarantee her silence.

But the thought of Del Toro being married to JoNell, even if only for a business arrangement, had obviously been too much torture for Consuelo. She had to have the satisfaction of telling JoNell she knew their secret, and to remind her that Jorge Del Toro was still Consuelo's property.

The evening's tension together with the ugly scene with Consuelo was too much for JoNell. She was beginning to feel ill. Her stomach had tightened into a knot, making her weak and breathless. She felt clammy, as if her blood had been drained from her body.

She moved away from Consuelo on shaky legs that threatened any moment to give way. For once, she was glad to catch sight of Del Toro. He was standing, drink in hand, with a group of men. But when he saw her, he put his drink down and walked swiftly to her side. "Are you all right?" he asked gruffly. "You look pale."

"I'm not feeling well," she confessed. "I think I need to lie down."

Without a word, Del Toro took her arm and led her out of the ballroom into the hallway. "The party has been a strain—"

She nodded numbly. He half carried her up the stairs and to her room. She sank gratefully on the edge of her bed.

"Lie down," he commanded.

She felt her cheeks burn scarlet, thinking of the implication of this bed and their wedding night.

"Lie down, I said," he ordered sternly.

Meekly, she lay back against the pillow.

"Let me loosen that for you," he said, reaching for the buttons on her lace bodice.

"No," she said quickly, using the small reserve of strength remaining in her. "I can manage."

"How do you feel? Shall I call a doctor?"

"No, I'll be fine. Just too much excitement and too much champagne," she lied.

He nodded. "I'll have the maid bring you some hot tea."

He started to the door. Suddenly, JoNell blurted out, "Consuelo told me she knows that you married me just because of my United States citizenship."

He turned slowly, his face darkened with a frown.

"I assume you told her," JoNell said.

He was silent for a moment, studying her face. His

eyes were shadowed. She could not see if they were angry or puzzled. Finally, he murmured, "Why would I do that?"

"Obviously to reassure her, so she'll be waiting for you when the year is up." Then JoNell shrugged. "It doesn't make any difference to me, except that you were so explicit about not telling anyone. Of course, what you tell Consuelo is your business."

"There is bound to be some gossip, some speculation. How do you know Consuelo wasn't just making a lucky guess?"

"Because of your relationship with her. It didn't sound like a lucky guess to me. It sounded like she had inside information."

"And that angers you?"

"Of course not," she snapped back. But then she amended, "Well, in a way it does. You want to be so all-fired secretive about the arrangement, then you go running to tell your girl friend."

"You resent Consuelo being my 'girl friend' as you put it?"

"It's a bit infuriating having her hovering around like a vulture counting the days until you discard me."

There was something else that she would never in a million years admit to him. It was the memory of the intimacy they had shared on this bed just a week ago, a memory that made her heart pound and her cheeks burn. A woman could not have reached such heights of physical passion with a man and not afterward feel some degree of possessiveness toward him, even if she did not love him.

There was a long moment's silence. Then Del Toro said, "I will make your excuses to the guests, and I will send the maid up with the tea."

He closed the bedroom door quietly as he left.

She wondered if he would now spend the remainder

of the party in the company of the lovely Consuelo, and if later they would seek the seclusion of the garden together. And she wondered why that thought brought stinging tears to her eyes.

Chapter 7

"A woman named Margarita will keep track of who gives you what," Del Toro said, giving JoNell last minute instructions as he helped her out of the Rolls Royce. "She's been here for a couple of hours, overseeing arrangements with the gifts. I want you to act as if you're having a good time."

"Yes, señor," JoNell said with mock obedience.

"It's your wedding shower. You'd be a fool not to enjoy it," he pointed out, as if logic were an antidote for her troubled feelings.

"And what am I supposed to do with all my gifts a year from now?"

She tried to avoid giving him her hand as she got out of the back seat. But he took it with an obvious air of authority, so she had no choice but to let him help her.

"Keep them. These people can well afford everything they give you and then some."

"That's not the point," JoNell countered. "I don't like accepting gifts under false pretenses."

He walked her to the door of the country club. "If it makes you feel any better, think of it as an excuse for the señoras to have a party. They love their hen parties, and then you've more than earned your presents by providing them with a new topic for gossip."

"You're despicable," she shot back.

He merely chuckled and opened the massive dark oak door for her with an exaggerated bow.

JoNell stepped inside, a shameful feeling permeating

106

her bones. She watched through a window as Miguel whisked Del Toro off to a business meeting. She felt utterly alone.

JoNell walked reluctantly through the foyer and into the main dining room. A crystal chandelier spread its soft glow over gold velvet wall covering. The soles of her black pumps sank into elegant carpeting. Her brown eyes darted anxiously around the crowd. Dark heads of classically styled hair bobbed all around the room, but one particular head of dark hair was visibly absent.

"I simply won't go if Consuelo is there!" JoNell had issued the ultimatum to Del Toro when he informed her of the wedding shower. "I can't take another round of her insults."

Del Toro had smiled as if amused by her discomfort. But he had assured her that Consuelo would not attend the shower.

"Señora Del Toro," said a voice as thin as a silken thread. "Welcome!"

JoNell was greeted by a young, bird-like woman with a long neck and a body as slender as a fashion model. She had piles of golden curls atop her head which made her appear quite out of place among the dark-haired Peruvians.

"My name is Margarita Sanchez. How nice to have another blonde among us."

"Thank you," JoNell said stiffly. She appreciated the woman trying to make her feel comfortable, but JoNell certainly did not feel "among" them. The word implied acceptance into their social group, but she knew she would never fit. It would take more than her designer dress of pearl-studded blue chiffon to transform her into a Peruvian socialite.

"We will have our tea first, and then you can open your presents," said Margarita. "If that is all right with you."

107

"Certainly."

The plum rose taffeta skirt swished in front of JoNell as she followed Margarita to a long table covered with an ecru colored table cloth. Each place setting contained a linen napkin in a silver napkin holder, silver service, and a crystal goblet of water.

"I think you know most of the ladies here," Margarita piped in her high register, "from your husband's party."

"Yes."

"My, I must say we were all quite surprised by Jorge's sudden marriage. Everyone's dying to get to know you—to find out what you have that we don't have."

JoNell felt her cheeks grow warm. Of course, some of the women at this wedding shower would probably at some time in the past have been romantically linked with Del Toro. It made sense. These were the women in his stratum of society. Not all of them were married. Some were daughters or sisters of business associates. She sank into her chair feeling even more self-conscious and ill at ease than before.

"Are you all right, señora Del Toro?" Margarita asked, fluttering around her like a bird.

"Yes, I'm fine," JoNell managed to say. "I—I just felt a little weak for a moment."

Margarita looked at her closely. "Perhaps you are going to enlarge the Del Toro clan before too long?"

"No, it's definitely not that!" JoNell protested, her cheeks growing even hotter. "May I meet the rest of the ladies?" she asked, trying to change the subject as quickly as possible.

"Of course."

Margarita clapped her hands for attention and introduced JoNell to the group of about fifty women.

In this ambience of elegant attire and cosmopolitan conversation, JoNell decided that the best way to avoid being conspicuous and calling attention to her lack of sophistication was to say as little as possible.

The preliminaries took about an hour. First the women were served steaming tea in individual silver pots. Then the waiters brought a crisp pastry filled with whipped cream. Finally, each guest received a small plate of assorted sliced fruits: chirimoya, banana and grapes. The women ate each delicate course languidly, their high-pitched chatter rising and falling, punctuated with peals of laughter.

JoNell was immensely relieved when the final plate had been cleared from the table, and Margarita announced it was time to retire to the lounge area.

The guests rose and moved past the sliding partitions that separated the dining room from the equally plush lounge area. Stacked in one corner was an embarrassingly large mound of gifts. JoNell had trouble swallowing.

"This is the place of honor," said Margarita, and guided JoNell to a green brocade upholstered chair. JoNell wondered if she detected a subtle note of sarcasm in Margarita's overly solicitous voice.

The other women took chairs around the room and sat expectantly. JoNell faced the sea of unfamiliar faces. The fact that she had met some of these women at Del Toro's party didn't make them any less strangers to her. She chewed the inside of her lip and tried to avoid their penetrating stares.

A woman named Pachia began handing JoNell presents while Margarita made a detailed list of the gift and the giver. JoNell hesitated over the first present. It was a large box wrapped in white with a huge, white bow. She felt a wave of bitter rebellion against accepting what she knew would be expensive items, when her marriage was a sham. But, again, as she found so often these days, she did not have a choice.

As JoNell opened the presents one by one, she

sensed a growing undercurrent of dissension among certain women in the room. She puzzled over this until Margarita whispered in her ear, "Now that they've sized you up, they're arguing over what you have that they don't have that made Jorge pick you over one of them."

JoNell tried to reflect her most pert smile, but inside she felt wretched. Not only had she been forced to endure the pain of a meaningless bridal shower, but she had been cast to the dogs to pick her bones clean. It was too much. The tears that she had felt on the brim of her eyelids the entire afternoon spilled over and trickled down her face.

She covered her face with her hands. A hush fell over the room.

"I do think she's overcome with happiness," piped Margarita.

Margarita's comment, combined with embarrassment at breaking down in front of a group of strangers, added more tears to the torrent.

Embarrassed coughs reached JoNell's ears. She fumbled in her purse for a lace handkerchief and dabbed at her eyes.

"I—I want to thank you for all these beautiful gifts," she choked. "You really shouldn't have," she said with an earnestness she hoped no one understood, "but I do thank you."

The silence broke again into little whirlpools of gossip as the crowd began getting up and mingling for their final goodbyes of the afternoon.

JoNell sat in her chair, too miserable to get up. She was congratulated again by several guests, mostly older women.

The crowd began thinning out slowly. JoNell occupied herself by looking at her expensive gifts, pretending to enjoy their beauty to cover up her self-recrimination. Only the knowledge that Del Toro had kept his word about the large cargo plane purchase to save her parents' business kept her playing this charade. When she thought of her mother's voice on the phone that morning, she told herself the price she was paying was worth it.

"JoNell, so much has happened!" her mother had bubbled over the phone, and she had dissolved into tears. "In fact everything would be just about perfect if I had been able to attend your wedding," she choked.

"I know, Mother. I'm awfully sorry about that. Jorge persuaded me to get married right away—and I knew you wouldn't be able to leave father anyway."

"Everyone is just ecstatic over your señor Del Toro. From what Uncle Edgar tells us, he's quite a catch."

"That's what everyone here says, too," JoNell replied, trying to keep sarcasm from her voice.

"Uncle Edgar told you about the enormous cargo plane purchase your husband has made through our company?"

"Yes."

"JoNell, do you know what that has meant to your father? He's regained his will to live. He went down to the airport this morning. It's the first time he's set foot inside the place since his heart attack. His doctor is so pleased. JoNell, only you can know what this means to us. Did you have something to do with it?"

JoNell swallowed hard. "It was strictly Jorge's idea," she said, trying to keep her voice level. "He said he needed the planes for a new cargo line he's setting up, and we might as well keep the business in the family."

"How sweet and generous! Please thank him for us, honey. He may not know it, but he's saved our business. He must be a fine and considerate man."

JoNell squeezed her eyes tight to well up a dam of bitter tears. How her mother would change her estimation of Del Toro if she knew the truth about the man!

"Crying again?" Margarita asked, breaking into

JoNell's thoughts. "I always thought of *Norte Americanos* as being less emotional than we Peruvians."

JoNell forced a weak smile. "Thank you for being so helpful," she said, reaching for the list of gifts Margarita had compiled.

"On the contrary," Margarita said with a gleam in her eye. "We should be thanking you."

"For what."

"For taking Jorge Del Toro out of circulation. You can't imagine the enemies he's created among the women fighting over him. Now that he's taken, life should be more peaceful in Lima."

JoNell winced. "I know about his reputation," she said calmly. "But a lot of it is pure exaggeration."

"Of course," Margarita smiled condescendingly. She paused. "If that is what you choose to believe."

JoNell didn't quite know what to make of Margarita. Perhaps the blond Peruvian had been one of Del Toro's conquests. Or worse still, for Margarita, maybe she hadn't! How furious she must be if she couldn't land Del Toro, but another blonde had. Perhaps Margarita's helpfulness had been designed to win JoNell's confidence so she would be in a better position to strike at JoNell's self-confidence with subtle innuendos.

JoNell experienced an overpowering urge to escape from the country club and get back to Del Toro's mansion. At least there, she knew where she stood. She had been bought and paid for, and there was no mistaking Del Toro's motives for marrying her.

JoNell excused herself as civilly as she could and hurried out to find Miguel leaning against the Rolls, waiting for her. He greeted her with a warm grin, opened the car door for her, and set about transporting the bridal shower gifts from the club room to the car.

That weekend, JoNell saw Jorge Del Toro in a new role, that of a polo star. She discovered that polo was a sport he pursued with great enthusiasm. Miguel drove her to the polo grounds where she had a seat that gave her an excellent view. It was the first time she had seen a live polo match. Whatever other feelings she had about Del Toro, she had to admit that he was a strikingly handsome figure astride a horse. His muscular shoulders and arms bulged against the white, tight-fitting polo shirt. He looked like a reincarnation of one of his fierce conquistador ancestors as he spurred his horse furiously down the field. She could see that he played the game of polo as he played the game of love and business—with ruthless determination to win. And win he did that afternoon. The other players were no match against the big, athletic conquistador who dominated his horse with fierce determination.

And that night, when he came to her bedroom, flushed with victory, he was again the ruthless conquistador, conquering the cold rebellion of her body until hate was transformed into passion—but passion that was short-lived, leaving her only the cold ashes of bitterness and regret at this charade of a marriage.

The next afternoon, JoNell sat half dozing on the veranda overlooking the garden, a magazine trailing from her slender fingers to the floor.

"Good afternoon, señora," a masculine voice suddenly said behind her.

She dropped the magazine and turned to meet deep black eyes in an angular face. It was Rafael Garcia, the persistent young man who had so ardently pursued her the night of the party.

"Señor Garcia! This is a surprise."

"A pleasant one, I hope. You are happy that I came?"

JoNell hesitated, groping for a way to field the question diplomatically. "It's always nice to see a friend of my husband," she murmured.

He indicated a black wrought-iron chair opposite her. "May I?"

113

She nodded, and he sat in the chair. "Am I not a friend of yours, too?" His penetrating gaze made her blush.

"We hardly know each other, señor."

"My heart tells me differently."

"Did you come to see my husband on business?" she asked, trying to change the subject. She remembered how persistent his overtures had been the night of the party.

"No, señora, I came to see you."

"Oh, that's too bad," she lied with a rush, rising from her chair, "I've just time to change before I have to leave for the country club. I have a golf lesson this afternoon."

"Forget the lesson this once." His hand reached out for her. "I came on a matter of great importance."

"Oh?"

"JoNell—I want you to marry me," he blurted out.

She stared at him, momentarily dumbfounded. Was he a mental case, she wondered with a flurry of panic. She could detect a slightly feverish look in his eyes.

"Señor, you know I am married," she stammered. "I have already made it quite clear that I am loyal to my husband."

"But you don't love him."

She stared at him with a blank expression, trying to maintain a grasp on the troubled emotions his words had stirred.

"Señor, this conversation has gone far enough. Now if you'll excuse me—" She rose to leave. "There is nothing more to discuss."

"Not even Consuelo Garcia?"

That stopped her dead in her tracks.

"And, perhaps you would like to know why she told you Del Toro married you just to get into the United States?"

JoNell sat down again, her knees weak.

114

"I am sorry to be so crude and blunt, but you were on the verge of leaving before I had a chance to explain some things I think you should know."

"What things?" JoNell asked faintly.

"Consuelo is plotting to break up your marriage to Del Toro."

"How do you know all these things?"

"I am Consuelo's brother, after all."

"Her *brother!*"

"Yes. You did not link our last names?"

"It didn't occur to me. Garcia is a very common name. And you look nothing like Consuelo."

"That is true. Consuelo is fair and I am dark." He smiled. "We always said she inherited the royal Spanish blood from our ancestors while I inherited the Inca blood."

JoNell tried to assimilate this bit of surprising information. "But why have you come here to tell me about Consuelo?"

"Because I truly love you," he said with great emotion. "When Consuelo found out about Del Toro's marriage to you, she was beside herself with anger and grief. She vowed to stop at nothing to get him back. She even persuaded me to help her. That's why I sought you out at the party. I'm ashamed to admit it now, but I followed you to the balcony to woo you for my sister's sake. She is my own flesh and blood sister, but I have to be frank and say she is a determined woman who will use any method to get what she wants."

"We'll agree on that point," JoNell said dryly. "And are you here now for her sake?"

"Oh, no!" he said emphatically. "Consuelo would scratch my eyes out if she knew I was telling you the truth. You see, not only does Consuelo want Del Toro for herself, but our family needs his money."

"His money? Whatever for? Your family is equally rich, is it not?"

"That once was true, but sad to say, it is no longer that way. The family fortune has dwindled over the years. Our name and reputation have provided us with a mantle of artificial wealth. We have clung to the hope that our fortune would be restored when Consuelo and Del Toro married. But then you came along—"

"And threw a monkey wrench in the works," she concluded in English.

"I did not want to be a party to wooing a woman away from her husband so my sister could have the husband," Rafael continued, using his native language. "But Consuelo was very persuasive. I finally agreed to try—but I got caught in my own trap."

"What do you mean?"

"When I saw you on the veranda, how delicate and lovely you were, I was glad I had agreed to my sister's plan. Then, as we talked, I sensed a special quality about you that I have never before found in any other woman. What started out as stock flattering phrases that roll easily off the tongue of any Peruvian man, turned into true expressions of my feelings for you. JoNell, I have fallen in love with you. My heart bleeds because you do not return my love. I want you more than you can imagine. I cannot offer you the riches that Del Toro has, but I offer you something he can never give you. My love. Del Toro does not love you. He loves no one but himself."

"Not true," she thought. "He loves Consuelo. And she knows it. But she is not content to wait out the year. Perhaps she's afraid he'll change his mind about her. She wants him *now,* and she wants his fortune for herself and her family. And she had the nerve to call *me* a gold digger!"

A cloud of mental confusion swept over JoNell. Conflicting thoughts wrestled in her mind. She had to admit to herself that she was attracted to the young man sitting opposite her. He was sincere, compassionate and kind, nothing like the egotistical Del Toro who thought nothing of buying another human being to serve his own purpose. With a man like Rafael, she would be loved for herself and cared for tenderly. It would be possible to grow to love a man such as this. But Rafael was not in a position to help her parents as Del Toro was. For their sake, she had to be practical and materialistic. Besides, she had made a pact with Del Toro, and she meant to keep her end of the bargain for the next year. Until the year was up, she would put all thought of love out of her heart.

"Rafael," she said as kindly as she could manage. "In other circumstances, I would be happy to have you care for me. But it is impossible. I am not the kind of person you think I am. I am not nearly good enough for you."

"Now you ridicule me," Rafael said sadly.

"No—not at all. I am highly flattered by your attention. But you deserve a finer person than I am."

"There is no finer person than you, JoNell!"

JoNell flushed. "Rafael, thank you for what you have told me—about your feelings and about your sister, Consuelo. What you have told me is important to me. But now I'm dreadfully tired. Please be kind enough to excuse me."

Reluctantly, he arose. "Very well. I'll leave you now. But I haven't given up. I'll be back. One day you'll realize the truth about Del Toro. When that time comes, I'll be there to claim you."

JoNell heard the door behind her open and close. The air felt suddenly cold and damp. Feeling threatened, she went inside and sought solace in her large, comfortable bed. She had just settled comfortably under a large, white afghan woven of alpaca when the door of the room opened, and in strode Del Toro.

His countenance looked dark and threatening. "I see you had company."

"Company?"

"Yes. Rafael Garcia. Don't deny it. I saw him leaving the house as I was returning from my business meeting."

She shrugged. "Yes, señor Garcia dropped by for a few minutes."

Del Toro scowled. "I don't want you entertaining men when I am not home. Gossip starts easily in this city. Our servants gossip to other servants, and the next thing there is a full blown scandal."

She raised her chin defiantly. "That is all you are concerned about—the honor of the Del Toro name? You are not interested in whether or not he made love to me?"

The storm clouds in Del Toro's eyes grew darker. "Did he make love to you?"

She met his eyes squarely. "He said he loves me. He wants me to divorce you and marry him."

There was a long, tight silence. Del Toro's eyes were like scalpels probing her gaze. "And what was your answer? Do you love him?"

She shrugged. "That's really no concern of yours, is it? That's my own private matter." She was silent for a moment, then added, "But you need have no fear of a scandal. You and I have a business agreement. You kept your part of the bargain—you ordered the cargo planes from my father and saved his business. I am grateful for that. And I fully intend to keep my end of the agreement. But after the year is up, who knows? Perhaps, after the divorce, I will marry Rafael. You will marry his sister, Consuelo. That would make you my brother-in-law. A relationship," she smiled, "that I would much prefer to the one you and I now have."

Again there was a deadly silence. Del Toro moved away from her to the window and stared moodily at the garden below. "I want you to pack a few things. Tomorrow we will fly to a village in the mountains

118

where I have a copper mine. We will be away two or three days."

JoNell was surprised and pleased. It would be a relief and welcome change of pace to get away from his artificial social world and behind the controls of an airplane again. '

"Just take casual wear," he said. "And a warm jacket. It gets quite cool in the mountains in the evenings."

"You do the navigating," she ordered brusquely as they buckled their seat belts in the plane. "You need the practice." She thrust into his hand a sectional map she had marked to show their course. "Are you sure there's a good place to land in this village?"

"There's an airstrip of sorts, primitive, but adequate. I've had chartered planes fly me there many times."

The flight to the village was breathtaking. She was used to the flatlands of southern Florida. Here the mountains rose majestically, the lofty peaks dissolving into mists. And below was the lush green jungle and rain forests. Fortunately, she had ferried some airplanes with her mother to customers living in mountainous regions, so she had learned the tricks of mountain flying. There were treacherous down-drafts swooping through some of the valleys, and it was crucial to fly high enough to avoid becoming their victim. She had to be alert not to let the awesomeness of the peaks fool her into thinking that she was further away from them than she was. Many an airplane had smashed into the side of a mountain from just such an error.

"What was our last checkpoint?" JoNell asked, glancing at the aerial map to see if Del Toro was accurately interpreting the colored squiggles and symbols. He had picked up an amazing amount of navigational skill along with his flying instruction. Most students were required to spend a considerable amount of time attending ground school to labor over details of navigating that Del Toro picked up with ease. Whatever else she felt about him, JoNell had to admit he had a brilliant mind.

"It's that mountain right over there," Del Toro replied to her question about the checkpoint. He nodded toward the peak and matched it up with its replica on the map.

"That means our ground speed is very good," JoNell commented. "That tail wind is pushing us faster than I had anticipated. We ought to be there soon."

The tension Del Toro had displayed during the first lessons had gradually eased until today she had found him almost completely relaxed on take-off.

"I have never really understood why you wanted to learn to fly," JoNell said. "It would be a simple matter for you to hire a pilot to fly you wherever you want to go."

"For a number of personal reasons," he shrugged. His evasive reply whetted her curiosity.

"Learning to fly must be very important to you. You found time for your lessons in spite of your hectic business schedule."

"Yes." His curt reply signaled the end of the conversation. But JoNell's frustration nibbled away at her. In spite of how she despised him, she could not stifle her curiosity. Why? At the moment, she did not know why. But something nagged at her to try and penetrate his exterior shell and get to the real man.

"Do you go to this village often?"

"From time to time," he said noncommittally.

It was obvious he had no intention of allowing himself to be cross-examined, no matter how subtly she approached him. The situation was trying her patience. For some reason, his refusal to be open with her was maddening.

She decided to be direct. "You are deliberately avoiding my question. Why?"

Cold orbs of steely green raked over a pert, fair-skinned face. "You really want to know something about me? Why?"

Why, indeed? Reason told her to let the matter drop. Instead, she persisted. "Why not? Like it or not, I am forced to play the role of your wife for the next year. I find it irritating when you are so darned mysterious. It might make things more comfortable if we knew a little more about each other."

His chuckle had a mocking quality that irritated her more. But he said, "Very well. What do you want to know?"

"First of all, why are we going to this remote village?"

"I told you. Business. I own a copper mine there. I check on all my operations personally from time to time."

"All right. Second, you have never given me a straight answer about why you wanted to take flying lessons when they made you so nervous. I asked you about that on the first lesson, and all you'd tell me was that it was a 'personal matter.'"

"Well, it was a personal matter, though there's no big mystery or secret about it. I really didn't think it mattered that much to you. You see, my parents were killed in a plane crash."

"Oh. I—I'm sorry," she stammered, at a loss to know how to respond.

"It was a long time ago. I was only fifteen. An aunt and uncle finished raising me. I was very young and impressionable. My parents were taken from me so unexpectedly, in the prime of their lives. They had so much to live for. Eventually, I learned to accept that they were gone. But I never got over how they died."

JoNell cleared her throat. Embarrassment over her first glimpse of an unexpected side of Del Toro's nature stilled her tongue. For the first time since she had met him, he seemed genuinely human.

Finally, her tongue came back to life. "No wonder you were so reluctant to have me teach you. You wanted more than just flying lessons. You had a crisis to resolve—a phobia about flying. When you saw what you thought was a mere girl, you couldn't even consider putting yourself in my hands."

"Until you gave me that first plane ride and demonstrated your skill," he chuckled.

"How did you have the nerve to go up with me?"

His gaze became icy, aloof. "You are never to doubt my courage. Jorge Del Toro fears nothing. The 'phobia' I had about flying, as you call it, was a weakness left over from my childhood. I despise weakness in a man. I was determined to conquer the problem by meeting it head-on, and I have."

JoNell decided it was a good place to drop the subject, though she was left with a grudging admiration for his courage. Del Toro was such an enigma. Just when she thought she was beginning to understand him, he showed facets of his character that surprised her.

"There it is," Del Toro exclaimed, pointing to a small cluster of buildings. JoNell glanced at the sectional map, surveyed the ground, and agreed that they had arrived. She circled the small mountain village, eyeing the "landing strip" Del Toro had described.

"That open stretch of meadow you call a landing strip is not very long," she said uneasily.

"With your skill, I didn't think it mattered."

"It matters, all right," she said curtly.

She made a low pass over the open field. A man tending about a dozen llamas looked up and began pointing and shouting. Several other men appeared from a grove of trees and they prodded the slow-moving llamas off to one side of the field.

JoNell made two more passes before the animals were clear of the "runway." She checked the sway of the trees and tall grasses to determine the direction of the wind.

"I don't like the length," she reiterated. "It's so short. We'll be cutting it close."

But Del Toro merely shrugged. "Land," he said.

"Okay; you asked for it." JoNell headed for the stretch of green pasture, coming in lower than normal. The wheels of the plane tickled the top of the tall grass that fringed the bare, flat ground. Once clear of the grass, she cut the throttle completely and pulled back on the stick. The little plane settled down comfortably and touched ground. JoNell braked the plane rapidly, her muscles tense. They ground to a halt just ten feet from the edge of the meadow.

"Beautiful!" Del Toro exclaimed. "I knew you could do it."

She saw tiny beads of perspiration shining on Del Toro's forehead. "You did that on purpose, didn't you—knowing it was a risky landing spot," she fumed. "It wasn't enough for you to learn to fly. You had to test yourself with some kind of danger in an airplane. And you chose me to do it with!"

"I told you, I despise weakness in a man," he said sternly.

At that moment, she didn't know whether to admire him or hit him with a wrench.

Del Toro opened his door and climbed out of the plane. She heard cries of "Del Toro! Señor Del Toro!" She saw a group of small, dark-skinned men rushing to embrace him. Each man in turn hugged him and patted him on the back—the Latin *abrazo* used by men who liked and respected one another.

JoNell got out of the plane on her side. She heard

Del Toro speaking to the men in the dialect of the Indian village. She realized these people were direct descendents of the Incas. They had their own language, quite different from the Spanish of Lima. Then Del Toro took her hand, smiled, and rattled off another round of unintelligible phrases. The men grew respectfully silent. They removed their straw hats and held them in front of them in both hands. Then each man presented himself to JoNell, spoke what must have been his name, and bowed to her.

"You have just been formally introduced as my new wife. Now no man in the village will dare show you anything but the greatest respect. You are safer here than in your own home. So relax."

"I didn't know my nervousness showed," she said with surprise. She was surprised, not because Del Toro showed concern for her feelings, but because he had noticed them at all. Until now, he had not shown that he was capable of discerning another's emotions. She had thought that he focused only on himself and that he was devoid of empathy.

Del Toro led JoNell through the tall grass then down a dusty path that brought them into a small settlement of adobe huts. Windowless, with earthen floors and crude wooden furniture, the huts were nestled close together. There was a sameness about the huts, all built in a rectangular shape with a crude chimney on one side. Naked children chased each other in games of tag. Most of the villagers were quite dark with Oriental facial features that gave some credence to the theory that ice age Asians had migrated to the Western world via a Bering Strait land bridge.

Women came to the doorways to smile and wave. Del Toro bowed to them. "The women here have not heard of 'liberation,'" he said. "They work as their ancestors worked many generations before them. They cook, grind their own corn in stone *metates* for the tortillas, wash their clothes in the river, and seem quite content."

"You'd like for all women to be subjugated like that, wouldn't you?" she said testily.

He merely looked at her and chuckled.

As they continued into the village, JoNell found herself tiring quickly. She began to breathe heavily. Her legs felt wooden.

"Do you want to rest?" Del Toro asked, becoming aware of her condition.

"Yes, thank you," she said a trifle breathlessly.

"It's the high altitude. You have to acclimate yourself gradually."

He led her to the stump of a tree, where she sat down with a sigh. She was startled by a sharp squawk. She saw a flash of bright green and yellow feathers in a nearby tree. "A parrot!" she exclaimed.

"Yes. They are plentiful here on the edge of the jungle."

After a brief rest, she said she was ready to continue. This time they moved at a much slower pace. Behind them, the group of village men still followed. Their ponchos woven of bright red, yellow and black yarn, which hung from their shoulders to their knee-length tan trousers, contrasted sharply with the somber expressions on their dark faces. They shuffled their sandaled feet smoothly along the dusty path.

Scattered among the adobe huts were some thatched roof cottages built of a dark red brick. Del Toro led JoNell to one of the cottages and opened a wooden door.

"This is home," Del Toro said.

"Home?"

"Yes. It's mine. This is where I live when I come to the village."

JoNell entered the cottage while Del Toro remained
125

outside to talk to the group of men who had followed them. Her white sneakers touched the same gray soil they had walked on outside. But inside the cottage, the earth had been swept clean so that the floor was hard and dustless. The structure was one large square room, primitive but very colorful. On one side was a bed made from rough wooden boards. The mattress appeared to be palm leaves topped with straw. An alpaca bedspread of a white and brown pattern covered the straw. A fireplace had been built into the rear wall. Several brick tiers decorated with brightly colored clay pots jutted out from the wall and apparently served as counter tops to prepare food. The seating space was adobe or brick surfaces built along the wall. A table of rough wood was placed before the seats. A wooly llama rug covered the center of the floor. Masks, tapestries depicting large birds and animals and llama rugs hung from the walls.

JoNell had never before seen anything quite like Del Toro's village cottage. As she moved around the room, becoming familiar with its furnishings, a sensation of relaxation and contentment spread through her. Whether the room had some kind of magical effect on her, or whether it was due to the altitude, she didn't know. She only knew that she felt more relaxed than she had at any time since arriving in Peru.

She walked over to the bed and rubbed her hand over the alpaca bedspread. It was smooth and soft. She sat on the bed, a smile crossing her lips at the thought of how out of place she looked in her powder-blue jump suit and white sneakers. She was a twentieth-century woman finding herself suddenly in a primitive setting of an earlier time. She stretched out on the bed, snuggling cozily into the soft cloud of the bedspread. Suddenly, she was very sleepy. She dozed briefly.

"I see you've made yourself at home," said Del Toro's voice, jolting her awake.

She opened her eyelids with an effort. The first thing she saw was a red and gold poncho topping tan breeches on a figure much taller and more robust than any of the natives she had seen.

"Why are you wearing that outfit?" JoNell asked, sitting up.

"These are the native clothes of the village," Del Toro said. "They are more comfortable and better suited for the village."

He tossed her some garments. "Put these on."

JoNell picked up a roughly woven red skirt and a poncho of yellow, red and green. On the floor by the bed were a pair of leather sandals.

JoNell looked nervously around the room. "There's no place to dress," she protested.

"You needn't worry about your modesty," he said sarcastically. "I'm leaving. There's a problem in the copper mine that I have to take care of immediately."

"When will you be back?"

"I don't know. But don't worry about finding your way around. A woman named Angelita lives just next door. She speaks Spanish. I've asked her to look after you."

With that, he strode out the door, leaving her to dress.

JoNell sat on the bed for a long moment. She was eager to explore this colorful village, but the altitude had sapped much of her strength. She decided to proceed slowly until she had adjusted to the rarified air, and took her time changing from her jump suit to the native clothing Del Toro had given her. She had smoothed her ankle length skirt when she heard a soft tapping on the door.

JoNell slipped the colorful poncho over her head and opened the door to a middle-aged, dark-skinned woman who had Mongolian features. The subtle, oriental slant of her eyes was striking. She was dressed in a yellow, ankle length skirt and had a black and red poncho draped over her shoulders. Covering her thick, black hair was a hat with a crown of straw. The hat's wide brim was covered with a green material.

"Welcome," she said with a warm smile. "My name is Angelita. I promised Jorge to look after you while he is gone."

"Come in," JoNell said. "He told me you were our neighbor." She liked this woman immediately. There was a warm earthy quality about her that was absent in the socialites she had met back in Lima.

"I want to welcome you with this tribal hat," Angelita said. Then she explained, "In these small villages, each region has its own distinctive hat. It's one of our most prized symbols of our heritage. As you see, the hats from our village have a wide green brim."

JoNell was surprised at Angelita's polish. She had expected a simple native girl, but this woman was obviously quite aware of a life apart from the village.

"Thank you," JoNell said. "It's very kind of you to offer me a gift so special." She took the hat which was a carbon copy of Angelita's and tried it on.

"It makes you look quite handsome," said Angelita. "As if you needed any help!"

"Now I'm sure I like you," JoNell laughed.

Angelita joined in the laughter. "Have you rested enough to see some of the village?" she asked.

"Yes, I think so."

"Jorge told me how the altitude affected you. The main thing to remember is to walk slowly. Life here never hurries, so you needn't worry about rushing around to see everything."

"You haven't lived here all your life, have you?" JoNell asked as the two women stepped out into the daylight. They began strolling easily down the dirt street.

"No, but I was born here, as was Miguel."

"Miguel?"

"Yes, Jorge's chauffeur. He's my nephew. You have met him?"

JoNell registered surprise. Now she realized how Miguel knew all about Del Toro's trips to this mountain village.

"Yes, of course I have met Miguel. But Del To— Jorge didn't tell me you were Miguel's aunt."

"He wouldn't." Angelita clucked her tongue. "Jorge is a great one for letting people find out things for themselves."

They passed a small, dark man sitting in front of his hut. His foot pumped rhythmically to spin a small potter's wheel. JoNell stopped to watch. The man smiled at them, revealing several missing teeth, but didn't interrupt his work.

"He's making pottery," Angelita said. "We sell our crafts to vendors in the large cities."

"Did you live in the city, Angelita?" JoNell asked, as she watched the clay ball take shape under the potter's skilled hands. He dipped his hands into a bowl of water often and kept the spinning clay wet. The clay spread out gracefully into a wide orb with a thin waist below a smaller orb on top. He worked rapidly and skillfully.

"For a while. I thought life there would be more rewarding. But after a time, I tired of it. Besides, the villagers needed me here."

"In what way?"

"I'm the schoolteacher. After Jorge gave us the money to build our school, the village wanted a teacher. But they didn't want an outsider. I was the most qualified, so I came back."

"Just like that without any regrets for leaving the city?"

"Oh, yes!"

"Are you married, Angelita?"

The woman's dark, expressive face grew sad. "I was;

my husband and little son were killed in an earthquake in the city."

"Oh, I'm terribly sorry. I could cut my tongue out for asking," JoNell said, her face turning pink.

"That's all right. You didn't know."

Another man emerged from the hut carrying a finished vase and an assortment of paints in earthenware pots. JoNell watched as he placed the large vessel on the ground and skillfully applied bright colors to form a pastoral scene depicting life in the village. JoNell was surprised at the deftness and speed with which the artisan created colorful parrots in a palm tree and filled in orchids and wild strawberries. Llamas, burros, and alpacas strayed across the vase to merge into the background.

"He's really talented," JoNell exclaimed.

"Most of our people are skilled in crafts," said Angelita. "It is another part of our heritage from the Incas. We owe them a great deal for the life we live today."

In spite of their primitive surroundings, JoNell sensed a great pride in these simple people. She could easily identify with their loyalty to their culture. She had felt much the same when Consuelo had attacked her middle-class background.

"Would you like to go to the market?" Angelita asked.

"I'd love to."

The two women strolled leisurely past the pottery makers. JoNell was thankful that Del Toro had insisted she wear native clothes. She would have felt terribly out of place in her blue jump suit. But dressed as a native, in spite of her obvious Caucasian features, she was beginning to feel a part of the small village. Much of the credit had to go to Angelita. Her friendliness helped JoNell relax and feel accepted.

The two women rounded a corner in the area where

the huts were situated and were confronted by a large, adobe structure with bamboo booths arranged along the exterior walls. Inside the building, the same kinds of booths were filled with produce, meats, fruits and various handcrafts. JoNell was impressed by a collection of dolls wearing the native costume. She wanted to buy one, but realized that Del Toro had forgotten to leave her any money. She didn't even know what the medium of exchange was here. In Lima, it was the sol, but here? She was too embarrassed to ask Angelita to buy a doll for her, even though she knew Jorge would reimburse her later. So she simply admired the dolls and walked on. Another booth held a collection of hand-painted gourds, rattles, drums, reed flutes and horns. Then they came to a jewelry booth. The delicate silver filagree impressed her.

"This looks quite expensive," JoNell said, holding up a particularly stunning necklace with a jade pendant.

"It is," Angelita nodded. She indicated the man behind the table. "He really doesn't expect to sell it here. Expensive items like this go to the large cities. He displays it for others to admire. The craftsmen derive much pleasure from competing for compliments on their work."

"Please tell him for me how gorgeous it is," JoNell asked. "It is truly exquisite."

Angelita jabbered in the strange, musical-sounding dialect to the jewelryman. He smiled broadly, bobbed his head up and down and jabbered something back.

Angelita translated. "He is quite happy that you like his work. He will make you a special price if you want to buy it." Angelita quoted JoNell a figure that made her head swim.

"Tell him thank you, but I better think it over," she said, not wanting to hurt the man's feelings.

Angelita relayed the message, and the man smiled and bobbed his head again.

"Would you like for me to help you select some vegetables and meat for supper?" Angelita inquired as they entered the food section of the market.

"Supper?"

"Yes, Jorge said you would be cooking for him." Angelita hesitated. "He said you would welcome my assistance, but I don't want to intrude, so if. . . . "

JoNell felt her expression change from wide-eyed shock to a grateful smile. "That was a look of desperation, not fear of intrusion," she explained. "I couldn't possibly cook a meal here without your help. I wouldn't even know where to begin. Everything is so different."

Angelita smiled. "Yes, different in a special way that I think you will enjoy."

"You are right. I don't know when I've been so relaxed."

Angelita helped JoNell pick out avocados, bananas, oranges, wild strawberries and a sack of wild rice. A stringy looking meat hanging on a hook in the open air was the only choice. JoNell asked for a slice off the hindquarter that looked a little redder than the rest.

"There are spices at the house and cooking utensils," Angelita explained. "But since we have no refrigeration, we buy our fruits, vegetables and meats fresh every day."

Their final purchase was a loaf of a hard-crusted bread. Angelita paid for everything with soles, the usual Peruvian money.

JoNell noted how each purchase was wrapped separately in what appeared to be large leaves and tied with a rough twine. Angelita took from under her poncho two woven shopping bags. They sacked their purchases and started home.

"What kind of a man is Del—Jorge, really?" JoNell asked, nibbling a succulent strawberry as she walked.

"You should know that better than I," Angelita said with gentle surprise.

JoNell caught her bottom lip with her teeth. Del Toro had warned her not to reveal their business arrangement to anyone.

"I have seen only the 'big city Jorge,'" she explained. "I was just wondering if he is so different in this small village."

"How fortunate that you will have the opportunity to find out now that you are here," Angelita said with a smile. "To us here, Jorge is the big *patron*, the big, kind boss. Without his copper mine, this would be the poorest of villages. It is our main industry. Many men of the village work in the mine. But Jorge does more than pay their salaries. He paid for our school; he pays a doctor to come to the village clinic to tend the sick once a month. He sends a dentist here, also. Whenever we have a need we can't take care of in the village, we know that our *patron*, Jorge Del Toro, will provide for us. He is our benefactor. Without him, the village would not be as happy a place to live."

JoNell was silent, puzzling over Angelita's words which were so much an echo of what Miguel had told her. It was hard for her to imagine Jorge Del Toro as a kind benefactor and hero to anyone. He had only shown her his selfish, ruthless nature. Unless Miguel and Angelita were in cahoots, there must be another side to Del Toro that JoNell had never seen. It was hard to believe that Angelita would lie to her. She seemed so genuine. Yet, she was the only person JoNell had spoken to in the village and might be the only one there who could talk Spanish. If that were so, JoNell would have only Angelita's word for Del Toro's kind deeds. For a reason she couldn't fathom, it was becoming increasingly urgent that she get to know the real Jorge Del Toro.

"Angelita, are you the only villager who speaks Spanish?" JoNell asked.

"Goodness, no. We have many who speak Spanish. They must in order to trade in the marketplaces in the large cities."

JoNell thought that would give her the opportunity to hear from others their view of the enigmatic Jorge Del Toro.

They arrived at the cottage. Angelita showed JoNell the spices in the colorful handcrafted urns she had seen on the shelves earlier. The most important spice was garlic, which was used in the preparation of rice, an obligatory dish at every Peruvian meal. The large, thick-skinned bananas—*plátanos*—were grown for cooking. JoNell tasted one raw and made a face at its stinging flavor.

Angelita got a blaze going in the fireplace and showed JoNell how to sear the stringy meat to prepare for slow cooking in water. The earthenware pots cooked amazingly well, distributing the heat evenly throughout the food.

The two women were chatting over the cooking supper when Del Toro arrived. "You ladies seem to be having a good time," he grinned. "What have you cooked up for a hungry husband back from laboring in the mines?"

JoNell turned to look at Del Toro. She had an odd sensation that she was looking at a stranger. A subtle change had come over him since they had arrived in the village. The hard lines around his mouth were softer. His frown had relaxed. Instead of looking peculiar in the native garb of the Indian village, he seemed quite comfortably a part of the village. His voice was lighter, more cheerful.

"Oh, Jorge," Angelita bubbled. "You have really done yourself proud. JoNell is delightful. I'm so glad you brought her with you so we could all meet her. She will make you a fine wife."

JoNell's cheeks grew hot. She averted her eyes and pretended to stir the meat. The phony marriage was a bad enough trick to play on Del Toro's shallow society friends, but JoNell felt utterly miserable at deceiving a sweet person like Angelita.

"Will you join us for supper, Angelita?" Del Toro invited.

"Thank you, no. I have invited a widower from across the village to join me tonight. I think you know him, Jorge. His name is Carlos Izquierda."

"Ah, romance," Del Toro teased.

"Could be," Angelita agreed lightly.

"Thank you for looking after JoNell."

"It was my pleasure. And now, good evening."

JoNell's stomach felt as if she had swallowed a Mexican jumping bean after Angelita left. Del Toro was uncomfortably close to her in this small hut. His powerful presence filled the structure and unnerved her. In Lima, in his mansion, the spacious rooms left breathing air. Even the airplane had not felt so unbearably intimate as this room. JoNell kept her eyes on the pots and pretended to be absorbed in her cooking.

"That smells very good," Del Toro said. He took a chair near her.

She braved a glance at Del Toro, dressed in the colorful village attire. It was the first time she had seen him in anything less casual than an imported suit costing hundreds of dollars. In the sparkle of his green eyes, she saw the reflection of the fire dancing merrily. He sat there with one arm draped over the back of his chair, looking at her with a soft smile on his lips. Something in this scene disturbed her and made her edgy. It was as if he were an ordinary work-a-day husband, home from his day's labors, waiting for his dutiful wife to serve him supper. But he was anything but an ordinary man in more ways than JoNell cared to enumerate. And she was certainly not his dutiful wife, at least not in the accepted sense of the word. What disturbed her the most and made her uneasy, she realized, was that she was not at all repelled by the domestic picture they made.

It must be her longing for her own home, she told herself. Nothing in Del Toro's sophisticated world in Lima had any connection whatsoever with the kind of life she had lived back home in the States. But here in this mountain village, where the people labored for their existence, JoNell felt more comfortable. Naturally, a domestic evening around the hearth would stir up nostalgic feelings for her home.

She tried to dismiss any thoughts that Del Toro might also feel at home here. He was too much of the sophisticate to feel at ease in these humble surroundings. Yet, the man was a baffling paradox. He was sitting there as relaxed as if he had no thought of time. Gone was the usual bustling urgency that characterized him. In its place was a serene contentment, a *mañana* attitude that puzzled her.

"Why do you come here?" JoNell blurted out.

"Where?" Her question drew Del Toro from some deep, private reverie.

"This village."

He rubbed one finger thoughtfully over his mustache. "Are you making conversation, or do you really want to know?"

"I really want to know."

"It's because I have everything—and I have nothing."

"I don't understand."

"I was born into a rich family. I attended the best

136

schools. I wore the best clothes. I thought I was happy. Then my parents were killed. After they died, all my money and power meant nothing to me. What good was money without the people I loved?"

Del Toro paused, then shrugged. "But I didn't know how to live any other way. And I had many responsibilities to the people who depend on me for their livelihood. In Lima, I am weighed down with the burden of my business empire. I have many social obligations which I can't escape. But here, in this village, I have a family, people who love me and care about me. When I go down to the mines, I am one of them. I can be myself."

JoNell was silent, trying to adjust to the mixture of feelings that his words had brought. He had given her a glimpse of a different and unexpected side of his life. The more she knew him, the more baffling he became, and the more difficulty she had defining what her true feelings were. At the moment, she was aware of a compassion toward him that conflicted with her anger and resentment.

"After supper, we shall go to the *paseo* in the town square," Del Toro told her.

They ate in silence. When the dishes had been cleared away, they stepped from the cottage into the darkness. As Del Toro had warned, the mountain nights were chilly, and she was grateful for the warmth of the poncho. Torches lighted their pathway down the dusty road toward the market square. The cool night air kissed her cheeks and ran its fingers gently through the long blond tresses that bounced softly around her shoulders. Birds squawked in the jungle that fringed the village. One side of the square was bounded by a large adobe church with a wooden cross growing from its roof. Circling the other three sides of the little town's plaza were small shops and stores. An old-fashioned watering trough for burros reminded JoNell of a set for a Western movie. A crowd of people of all ages had gathered to sit on wooden benches in the center of the plaza. Chaperoned señoritas strolled around the square, smiling coquettishly and giggling at the young men who flirted with them. Small children played in and out of the crowd.

JoNell was acquainted with the Latin custom of the *paseo*, the evening stroll around the town square, where the young people, under adult supervision, had an open opportunity to meet, talk and begin courtship. Parents admired each other's children and chatted about the week's activities.

This was JoNell's first opportunity to actually participate in a real village *paseo*, and she was enjoying the experience. There was a warmth and community spirit in the custom that other cultures lacked.

A little boy about five years old, wearing ragged knee-length breeches, walked up to JoNell and presented her with an orchid. "Why, thank you," she exclaimed, but the blank look in the boy's large, black eyes, told her he didn't understand her Spanish. "Translate, will you?" she asked Del Toro.

Del Toro and the boy exchanged comments in the native language. The child stood looking up at JoNell.

"He wants to know if he can touch your hair," Del Toro said. "He's never seen anyone with 'yellow' hair before."

JoNell smiled at the choice of words. "Sure you can," she said, bending down so the little boy could stroke her hair.

The little face beamed with a gleeful smile and he shot off into the dark.

"What scared him off like that?" JoNell asked.

"Oh, he'll be back."

"You think so?"

"You can count on it."

"How do you know?"

"I know what he has in mind," Del Toro said with a mysterious chuckle. "And when he comes back, he won't be alone."

"Does he want to get me another flower as a reward for my letting him stroke my hair?"

Del Toro only smiled indulgently.

"No? Then I simply can't imagine."

JoNell followed the direction Del Toro's green eyes were looking, and she saw a tight little knot of boys jabbering in high-pitched tones.

Then, one by one, they solemnly approached. As each one handed her an orchid, he indicated he wanted to touch her hair. JoNell was struck by their gentle awe as they reached for her hair. She also accumulated a large lapful of purple orchids.

JoNell was touched by the ceremony. "How sweet that first little boy was to be so considerate of his friends," JoNell commented.

"How so?" Del Toro asked.

"Well, he told his friends about me, and had each one bring me a flower so I would let them touch my hair. That was a fine example of sharing."

"You think so?" Del Toro said with a laugh.

Then Del Toro said, "Hey, *muchacho*, come here." He repeated the command in the boy's native language. The first boy slowly approached. Del Toro rattled off another command.

The boy hung his head. Slowly, he extended one grimy fist. He opened his hand, showing them a palm full of *centavos*. Then he clamped his fist around the pennies and sped off into the night.

"Why that little con artist!" JoNell gasped. "You mean he was charging his friends to touch my hair?"

Del Toro was laughing heartily. "Exactly! I heard

them talking among themselves. Your little admirer told all his friends that they would have a lifetime of good luck if they touched your yellow hair. Furthermore, he claimed to have the 'hair-touching' concession, and only if they each gave him a *centavo* would he arrange with you to let them touch your hair."

JoNell joined Del Toro in laughing.

"He'll go far," Del Toro said, wiping tears of laughter from his green eyes. "I'll have to put him to work in one of my companies when he grows up."

"He'll probably organize the workers and take over," JoNell warned.

"He'd wind up chairman of the board at least."

They laughed together, looking into each other's eyes. JoNell felt a sudden warmth suffuse her, felt a catch in her throat. Her heart was beating in a strange, irregular way. She couldn't seem to pull her gaze away from her husband's eyes.

My husband—never before had she used those words in her own mind. But now she thought them, and repeated them. "My God," she thought, "what is happening to me." And even as she asked herself the question, she knew the answer. She was in love with Jorge Del Toro.

When had it happened? Tonight, when for the first time she saw him as a human being? Just this moment, when they shared laughter that broke down the wall of defenses? Or had it really happened the first time he strode into her life at the airport, a huge, masterful, totally masculine man?

There was no denying the overwhelming attraction she had felt for him from the first moment. She had hated him violently—but wasn't hatred a powerful emotion linked to powerful passions?

Yes, she had felt passion for him from the first. His kiss that day they landed on the deserted beach had fired raging passion in her that had never before been awakened. The same passion had racked her body on their wedding night. She had tried to keep that hunger of the flesh isolated from her heart and her soul. But tonight the isolation had ended and the warmth and love she felt for this baffling man suffused her entire being. Now he was no longer an enigma, no longer a cold, aloof, ruthless stranger. He was what her heart told her . . . *my husband.* . . .

"It's time for the married couples to join in the *paseo*," Del Toro said. He offered her his arm. She lay her hand across it, and they arose. She suddenly felt shy with him. She kept her eyes averted. A tingle raced through her. It was the first time she touched him knowing that she loved him.

As if in time to inaudible strains of music, married couples and courting sweethearts drifted around the square, holding hands and renewing their love for each other. JoNell's heart was breaking. She was being escorted around the square by a man she had just realized she loved—a hopeless love that would never be returned. Bittersweet agony threatened to squeeze the life from her heart. She hadn't known she could experience such emotional pain.

Del Toro was silent as they walked, off in a world with his own thoughts. No doubt he was thinking of his childhood sweetheart, Consuelo, wishing that she were by his side.

She began shivering.

"Is something the matter?" he asked.

"Yes. I'm cold. Could we go home, please?"

"You aren't enjoying the *paseo?*"

"No," she said, drawing away from him. "It makes me feel like a hypocrite. These married couples around us are in love. I feel like a trespasser."

His green eyes became angry. The relaxed feeling of

good humor between them dissolved. They walked back to the cottage in stony silence.

The next morning, Del Toro was gone when JoNell awoke. She dressed slowly and sat staring out the window, depressed and forlorn. Then Angelita appeared outside.

"Good morning," called the dark woman. "Altitude still getting you down?"

"Yeah, a little, I guess," JoNell lied.

"It takes a few days to adjust," Angelita said. "I'm going to the market. Want to come along? We'll take it slow and easy."

"Angelita, you're a jewel. That's just the medicine for what ails me."

The two women took the same route they had followed yesterday, but this time JoNell felt no joy in seeing the pottery maker, the glass blower, and the painter. Angelita did most of the talking.

When they returned, Angelita helped JoNell with the food preparation.

"You are troubled," Angelita observed. "It's Jorge, no?"

JoNell gave Angelita a startled look. Was it that obvious?

"Do not worry," Angelita said as she peeled a banana. "It will blow over. I know you have not been married long. There will be fights at first, but they will grow fewer and less intense. You cannot live with a man like Jorge Del Toro without great depths of feeling that sometimes erupt in anger."

"You seem to know Jorge very well," JoNell said, careful not to reveal the true nature of her dismay.

"Yes, I know him well. I was married to a man just like him," Angelita said with a smile.

"Were you happy with him, Angelita?"

"Oh, yes," she said softly. "Immensely happy. But

142

the marriage was stormy at times. Men like Del Toro have deep emotions. They have fire in their veins. They have much passion. They are quick to anger, but they also love deeply."

JoNell couldn't stop the swell of tears that trickled down her cheeks. She wished she could unburden her heart to this kind woman, but that was not possible. She had to keep her heartache a secret.

"There, there," Angelita soothed, taking JoNell in her arms. "Believe me, this fight has not ruined your marriage. Tomorrow all will be sunshine again."

No, thought JoNell. Tomorrow and all the tomorrows after that will change nothing. I'll be in love with Jorge, while he impatiently waits out the year so his business will be secure in the States and he can divorce me and go back to his childhood sweetheart, Consuelo. She will win out in the end, just as she warned me. What a fool I am. I fell into the trap I promised myself I would avoid. Chalk up another victim for the great Jorge Del Toro, breaker of women's hearts!

JoNell cried until there were no more tears left in her, and then she dried her eyes stiffly. She felt drained now. Her heart would hold room for nothing but a single-minded purpose. She would avoid Del Toro as much as possible and steel her heart against her love for him until her year as a wife had served his business purposes and the divorce ended this mock marriage.

That evening, JoNell said as little as possible to Del Toro when he returned from the mine. For the most part, they ate in silence. JoNell replied to his comments with short, curt answers.

After supper, he said, "There's a special tribal ceremony tonight being given in our honor. I can tell you are not in a festive mood. But it would be an insult to the village not to attend."

"Why in our honor?" she asked.

"Because we are newly married."

"You mean this phony marriage of convenience?" she said bitterly. "I think it would be a greater insult if we did attend."

"These people do not know the circumstances of our marriage," he said, his jade green eyes sparking anger. "You may never desire to come to this village again, but I intend to come back. I will not be rude to these people."

"Very well. I have no wish to be rude to them, either. I'll go for Angelita's sake," JoNell said, thinking that her friend would believe she and Del Toro had patched up their 'lover's quarrel.' She couldn't bear to disappoint someone who had been so kind to her.

They walked by torchlight to the town square. A crowd was gathering. A small man smiled broadly and directed them to the seat of honor, two large wooden chairs.

As soon as they had taken their places, JoNell heard the low pitched rumble of drums. From out of the darkness walked a small group of men playing gourds, drums of various sizes and shapes, and rattles. They began to wail in a high-pitched tone, bowed in unison, and then backed away from the spectators and sat in a semicircle in the shadow of the torchlight. Next came about a half dozen men in bright red trousers and multi-colored shirts with geometric designs emblazoned on the front and back. They wore weird headdresses of devils, birds, serpents and other animals. These were the dancers. In time to the compelling rhythms, they jogged, three jumps forward and two jumps back. They circled and changed places.

"What does that dance symbolize?" JoNell asked.

"It's a special feast dance. It is rarely performed for outsiders. They are paying you a great honor."

"It's certainly delightful. So colorful and rhythmic.

144

Makes me want to clap my hands." JoNell began to enjoy herself and forgot for a while the bitterness she felt for the man sitting next to her.

The drums stopped abruptly. A man emerged from the night playing a lonesome one-note melody on a reed-like instrument. A small, dark woman with her hair in a tight knot on her head and dressed in a long, white gown, stepped gracefully into the foreground. After each footstep she raised on her toes, paused, her eyes downcast, and then took another step. She was followed by a young man dressed in a simple black outfit. A woman's thin, high voice began to moan a sorrowful song.

"What's this?" JoNell asked.

"It's the *yaravi*. It's a song and dance about love."

JoNell felt a wave of panic. She didn't want to sit here watching a ritual love dance while she was acutely aware of Del Toro's broad shoulder brushing against hers. But she was trapped. There was no escape for her.

The young girl in white moved slowly around the arena, tossing orchids from a basket she had picked up from the ground. The young man followed her, always just beyond arm's reach, his hands extended as if trying to catch his elusive love object. He picked up one of the flowers she had dropped, buried his face in it and appeared to be crying.

The two dancers continued their ritual until at last the young woman appeared to notice the young man and offered him an orchid. He took it and began dancing exuberantly to the beat of excited drums. The girl stood by looking demure. Then the man scooped the girl up in his arms, and carried her away into the night.

"That's how love should be," JoNell thought dismally.

145

"This is the *huanyo,* a song and dance for couples," said Del Toro as a new group of performers moved into the torchlight.

By now JoNell was too miserable to enjoy the show. She scarcely noticed the bright turquoise and silver dresses of the women and the black and red trousers of the men. The lively music and intricate dance were wasted on her. She had no idea when she came here tonight that the festive dances would be such compelling symbols of love and touch such a vulnerable spot in her heart.

How hypocritical she felt! Everyone in this village thought her marriage to Del Toro was genuine, and they were doing their utmost to try and please her by celebrating her wedding. But what the village thought was love binding her and Del Toro together was nothing more than a business contract.

When the dances ended, Del Toro helped JoNell from the chair and they started back to their cottage. A short distance away, JoNell spied Angelita who was being escorted by a man who JoNell assumed was Angelita's widower. The woman winked, waved and smiled. JoNell forced herself to respond with a smile. There was no point in letting Angelita know how miserable she was.

When they were back at the cottage, Del Toro told JoNell that they would be leaving the village the next afternoon. She reacted with a mixture of relief and regret. There would always be a special corner of her heart reserved for memories of this village and its simple, warm-hearted people.

"Before we leave, I have something for you," Del Toro said. He handed her an object wrapped with a large leaf.

JoNell recognized the wrapping as the type used at the marketplace. She opened the package. A gasp escaped her lips. It was the exquisite necklace she had admired the day she and Angelita had toured the market!

"I see you've been checking up on me with Angelita," she said.

"What do you mean?"

"She's the only one who could have told you I admired this necklace in the marketplace."

"Then you do like it?"

"Yes, it's beautiful. But you needn't have gone to the trouble," she said tonelessly.

The necklace was like all the flowers he had sent her—merely a gesture with no real meaning. It was his way of paying her for the role she was playing.

She said, "I don't need to be paid for my services here in the village. When I married you, I agreed to pretend our marriage was authentic. You've already paid me by buying those airplanes through my father's business. You don't have to pay me again for doing my job." The look she gave him was hard and resentful.

Del Toro's eyes smoldered with dark fires. "Well, I thought you deserved something for the overtime you've put in," he snapped ironically.

"There's not enough jewelry in all of Peru to pay me for my 'overtime' as you so crudely put it."

They exchanged looks of bitter fury. They were strangers again, cold and distant. Del Toro stalked out of the hut, slamming the door with a resounding thud.

Tears sprang to JoNell's eyes and spilled over. She looked at the silver necklace and drew it to her bosom. How she would cherish it if Del Toro had given it to her because of his love for her. She would put it on and never take it off. She would be the happiest woman who ever drew breath. But instead, the necklace began to burn her palm. She tossed it on the bed as if it had suddenly become fiery. She glared at it. It symbolized the painful situation she was in. In her emotional state, she thought the lacy filigree began to resemble a pit of serpents, writhing in a mocking reflection of her heartbreak. Suddenly she hated the necklace and she hated Del Toro for giving it to her.

Chapter 8

JoNell had settled down at the desk in the study to draft a letter to her parents when she heard Maria, the maid, answer the front door. There was a murmur of voices. Then Maria came to the study door. "It is señor Rafael Garcia. He asks to see you."

JoNell nibbled at her lower lip. Del Toro would be angry if she allowed Rafael to visit her—and yet, she thought rebelliously, why not? Her sagging morale needed a boost. She had been miserably depressed since the trip to the mountain village.

She nodded to Maria.

"Hello, señor Garcia," she smiled when Maria showed him into the room.

"Señora Del Toro. It is a pleasure to see you again." He bowed politely and kept his greeting formal for the benefit of the maid, but the adoration in his eyes brought a flush of warmth to JoNell's lonely heart.

"Maria, would you please serve us tea in here?"

"Yes, señora."

Rafael waited until the maid had left the room. Then he took a chair close to JoNell's. His gaze lingered on her face. "JoNell, it is so good to see you. I phoned several times—"

"We spent a few days at a mining camp. We've been back for a week, though."

"I know." His dark eyes were brooding somberly. "I

keep in touch with your whereabouts. I knew you had returned to the city, but I had made up my mind not to try and see you any more. It was a decision my mind made, but my heart could not keep as you see."

She smiled at him fondly. "Rafael, what am I going to do about you? You know the situation is hopeless. I've tried to make that clear to you."

"I know," he sighed. "But again, it is my mind that listens, not my heart." He was thoughtful for a moment, his brooding eyes studying her face. "No, perhaps my mind, too, has doubts. Somehow, I just can't be convinced that you are happy with Jorge Del Toro. There is always a look of sadness in your eyes; not the radiant happiness of a new bride—"

JoNell flushed, glancing down at her fingers.

Fortunately the maid interrupted them with the tea tray. As Maria was arranging the dishes, JoNell made casual conversation. "How are you occupying your time these days, señor Garcia?"

"Oh, I have started a new job. My cousin has a Mercedes Benz dealership. He decided with my country club membership and social contacts, I would make a good salesman. Those are the kind of people who buy expensive cars. So far my commissions have been better than I expected."

"Good for you. Congratulations!"

The maid left. Rafael munched a pastry, his eyes thoughtful and brooding again. "Yes, soon I could support a wife. Not, of course, with the wealth of a Jorge Del Toro—"

His meaning was quite clear. Again JoNell's cheeks flushed. "Rafael, it is not fair for you to have such hopes—"

"Tell me honestly how you feel about me, JoNell."

"Honestly?"

"Yes . . . truthfully. Do not spare my feelings."

She had to think for a moment. Her emotions had been so confused since the trip to the mountain village, she could not answer such a question easily. That she was in love with Jorge Del Toro was a painful fact she could not escape. And that her love was not returned was an equally painful fact. And in the midst of that emotional turmoil, how did she feel about Rafael Garcia? She searched her heart and gave him the most honest answer she could find. "You are a fine person, gentle, kind, considerate. I am quite fond of you, Rafael."

He brooded over her reply for a moment, then said, "At least I have that much. Is it a fondness that could grow into love some day?"

She hesitated. "I—I honestly don't know at this point, Rafael. I'm afraid I'm mixed up, confused about a lot of things."

"I'm not going to give up until I know it is hopeless," he said stubbornly.

Impulsively, she rested her hand on his. "Could we be friends for now, Rafael? I do need a friend."

"Of course I am your friend. Confidant, companion, big brother, friend, lover—I will be what you want me to be. Just tell me. What I wish, of course, is to be your lover and your husband. But I can be patient. I have felt certain from the beginning that your marriage to Del Toro is not a happy one and it is destined to end in divorce. Several things have happened lately that strengthen that belief, and when the time comes, I will be waiting."

She looked at him quizzically. "What do you mean, 'several things have happened lately'?"

"The look in your eyes today for one thing. You are a new bride. You have just been off on a romantic trip with your husband to an isolated mountain mining camp. You should be singing and radiant. But when I look into your eyes, what do I see? Only loneliness and sadness—"

She glanced away. "Perhaps you should not look so deeply into my eyes," she whispered.

"And Del Toro—he does not act like a devoted husband. You do not see much of him, do you?"

She frowned. "How do you know so much about it?"

"You forget I have known Jorge Del Toro since childhood. We live in the same social world, have the same friends and business acquaintances. We are even distantly related, third or fourth cousins, I believe. At any rate, I know a great deal about where Jorge goes and what he does, probably more than you do, JoNell. In our culture, the man's world is separate from the woman's world. A man's friends or acquaintances may know more about his daily life away from home than does his own family."

"What are you trying to tell me?"

"What I said, that Jorge spends very little time at home with you."

"It's true I haven't seen him much since we got back," she admitted. "He has many business matters that take his time."

"Yes, business, and other matters."

She frowned at him. "What does that mean?"

He hesitated. "I should not have said that. It will only make me appear small in your eyes. And yet, I do not like to stand by and see you hurt and betrayed by a husband who cares nothing for you."

She felt a sudden tightness and pounding in her temples. "What—what do you mean, 'betrayed'?"

Rafael hesitated again. He looked down at his hands, spreading them on his knees. He shook his head slowly. "Forgive me for being the one to tell you this, JoNell. But I must. Jorge has been seeing my sister, Consuelo. They have met for cocktails in the afternoon. Once they had dinner in a secluded restaurant where he used to take her before he married you."

The blood drained from JoNell's face. She felt as if her heart had been impaled on a sharp spike. In that first moment she could only feel humiliation and hurt. Anger would come later.

"I'm sorry. I know you are upset. But I can't help but think Consuelo is right. She's convinced in her mind that Jorge married you because he needed an American wife for business purposes. She thinks it's a temporary situation, and she'll eventually get him back. Maybe he's even told her that. At any rate, she's very determined and very sure of herself."

JoNell arose and walked slowly to a window. She looked out at the garden through a haze of tears. Rafael had only confirmed what she'd known in her heart all along. But for another to confirm the truth hurt unbearably. If only she hadn't fallen in love with Jorge! What a hurtful trick her treacherous heart had played on her!

"JoNell," Rafael said gently. He had risen and moved behind her. Now she felt his hands on her shoulders. "I must go, but remember I am always close by if you need me. Whatever you need, whatever I can give you, you have only to ask me."

She nodded numbly.

"JoNell," he said huskily, "that first night on the balcony, I begged you for just one kiss, remember? I want to ask you again. It is a selfish request that comes only from my lonely heart."

How well she knew the meaning of an empty, lonely heart! How could she deny another heart in pain? She raised her face to his. For a long moment their eyes met, and then she closed hers, offering her lips. His mouth was warm and eager against hers.

She truly wished Rafael would awaken the trembling passion she felt in Del Toro's embrace. But after what

Rafael had told her about Del Toro and Consuelo, she felt nothing except numbness.

"My loved one," Rafael whispered. "I know there is no passion in your kiss for me. You are too decent a woman to be married to one man and feel passion for another, even if you do not love the man who is your husband. But your kiss gives me hope. It will give me reason to live until the time comes when you grow to love me."

He clasped her hands in his, kissing them. Then he was gone.

JoNell spent the remainder of the day aimlessly wandering around the mansion, her thoughts chaotic, her emotions storm-swept. Rafael's news that Del Toro was secretly seeing Consuelo should have come as no surprise. Nevertheless, it had forced her to face abruptly the cold reality of Del Toro's love for his lifelong sweetheart, and JoNell's position as an outsider. And that reality hurt more than she had imagined it would.

Late that afternoon, Maria brought her a message that deepened her anguish. "Señor Del Toro phoned, señora. He asked me to tell you that a pressing business matter has called him out of the city overnight. He will be back tomorrow."

JoNell stared at her dully. She drew a breath that was painful and nodded. "Thank you, Maria."

Why did he bother to make up such lies? He had made it clear from the beginning that he owed her nothing in this marriage except the financial arrangement with her parents, and she, in return, only had to pretend to the world that she was his wife. Did he feel guilty, having consummated the marriage, to be going to another woman? She supposed even a man as ruthless as Jorge Del Toro could have a conscience.

In any case, she knew that the "pressing business matter" that kept him away from home tonight was another tryst with Consuelo. Would she know the passion in his arms tonight that had been JoNell's those nights he had come to her bedroom?

The thought burned in her breast with throbbing despair.

That night, she cried herself to sleep on her lonely pillow. And when she awoke, the feeling of loneliness was close to a sensation of panic. She was alone in this huge mansion, alone in the city of Lima. She felt like a lost child in a strange and hostile forest.

She needed desperately to hear the voice of someone who loved and cared about her. Suddenly she found a telephone in her hand, heard herself putting in a long distance call to Florida.

When her mother's voice came on the line, JoNell had to make a superhuman effort to keep from bursting into tears.

"JoNell!" her mother exclaimed. "How good to hear your voice. Is everything all right, honey?"

JoNell swallowed hard. She took a slow, deep breath. Somehow she made her voice sound cheerful—a bit of acting that could have won her a drama award. "Everything's just fine, Mother," she said brightly. "I was feeling a little homesick . . . wanted to hear your voice. . . ."

"Well, we miss you, sweetheart."

"How's Daddy?"

"Oh, so much better. He's more like his old self every day. You know how he used to like to joke and tease all the time. He's trotting out all his old corny gags, and I'm pretending to laugh at them again. I really am laughing, not at the jokes, but because I'm so happy for him," she chuckled.

Tears were beginning to trickle down JoNell's cheeks. "How's the office, and the hangar, and my little plane? And that old striped alley cat that hangs around—?"

"Everything's just like you left it, honey. Uncle Edgar was tinkering with your plane yesterday, giving it a tune-up. The alley cat had kittens. Oh, and we're going to have a party."

"A party?"

"Yes, you know this week is our wedding anniversary. I thought we'd decorate the house up a bit and have a few friends and relatives over. I really feel in a festive mood. I just wish you could be here—"

JoNell's breath caught in her throat. "I will be there!"

"What?"

The blood was suddenly pounding in her temples. She wiped the tears from her cheeks with the back of her hand. In a rush she said, "Yes. I mean it, Mother. I'm going to fly home for a visit. . . ."

Yes, she would throw a few things into a suitcase and go straight to the airport. With luck, she could be home tonight, close to the people and surroundings she had known since childhood. She would feel safe and loved again.

"JoNell, do you really mean it?" her mother was babbling excitedly. "Oh, that would make everything just perfect! But how about your husband? He's coming too, isn't he?"

JoNell had to do some fast thinking. "Jorge is very busy right now, Mother. As you know, we're planning to move to the States. But he has a lot of business matters to wind up before we can make the move. He urged me to go ahead and fly home for a visit—"

She crossed her fingers as she told the fib. But after the monstrous lies she had told about her marriage, this seemed a very small untruth.

"He must be the most considerate husband in the world. You're so lucky, JoNell!"

Again tears seared her eyes. "Lucky?" she whispered.

"What, dear?"

She blinked away the burning tears. "Nothing, Mother. Listen, I'm going to the airport right now. If I'm lucky, I can get a flight out before noon. I'll call you from the airport and tell you when we'll reach Miami. Okay?"

"Yes. Okay, dear. You let us know. We'll be at the airport in Miami, waiting for you. Oh, I'm so excited!"

"Me too, Mom. Listen, kiss Daddy and Uncle Edgar for me. And the cat."

"Daddy and Uncle Edgar, okay. I don't know about the cat!"

They both laughed, JoNell a little hysterically. Then she hung up.

Feverishly, she threw some of her barest necessities into her flight bag. She took nothing that Del Toro had bought for her, except her engagement and wedding rings. In that matter she had no choice. Then she scribbled a note for Del Toro. She explained that she was homesick, it was her parents' anniversary, and she had decided to fly home for a few days. She couldn't resist including, with a wave of anger, a line saying that she was sure he would have plenty of company and wouldn't miss her.

She pinned the note to her pillow. Then she phoned for a taxi. She wanted to slip out of the house without the maid seeing her. Fortunately, Miguel had taken the cook to the market, so there were no other servants around, except for the gardener and he was busy in the greenhouse.

JoNell waited in the street for the taxi. When it arrived, she climbed in, pulled her bag in beside her, and stared sadly at the big mansion as they drove away. She had never known such a mixture of apprehension, sadness and relief all mixed together to form a pounding in her head. Perhaps when she was home, in her own environment, she could think more clearly about what was happening to her and decide how she was going to deal with her feelings for Jorge Del Toro for the remainder of their "marriage." Right now she was too confused by conflicting feelings of love and hate to know what to do about this man in her life who had turned her world upside down.

On the way to the airport, JoNell was so immersed in her torment that she scarcely noticed the unusually light flow of traffic in the city. The sidewalks were almost deserted. Many stores were closed, some of them with locked, iron gratings. Then she realized they were passing a lot of army trucks. She saw soldiers on every street corner. The taxi driver flicked on his radio. An excited announcer's voice was giving news bulletins. Over the taxi driver's agitated epithets, JoNell was able to make out that there had been a sudden military coup. The army, opposed to Geraldo Gustamente, had seized control of all radio and television stations and was moving swiftly to take over the government and impose a military dictatorship.

The taxi driver drew up to the airport and let JoNell out while still cursing under his breath. JoNell paid the man, then grabbed her bag and hurried into the terminal. There she was met with a scene of consternation. People were gathered in tight knots, talking excitedly. The air was brittle with tension. Crowds were milling around ticket windows. Some irate persons were waving fists over the counter. One woman, nursing a tiny baby, was crying. A general sense of chaos filled the terminal.

At the ticket counter, JoNell discovered the cause of the disturbance. The airport had been closed because of the sudden bloodless military revolution. There would be no flights of any kind, in or out of the country, for an indefinite period. She also learned that all other forms of transportation out of the country had ground to a standstill because of the unstable government situation.

JoNell was stunned by this totally unexpected turn of events. For a while, she became one of the lost souls, wandering around the terminal in a daze as she attempted to cope with this new frustration. Finally, in black despair, she returned by taxi to Del Toro's mansion.

Her leaden feet carried her unwillingly up the stairs to her room. She opened the door to find Del Toro standing near her bed, her note in his hands. His face looked like a thunderstorm about to happen.

She dropped her bag on the floor and collapsed into a chair, avoiding his gaze. She felt inutterably weary.

"So you have come back," he said with obvious agitation. He began pacing the room in angry strides.

"The airport is closed," she said dully.

"I know. You did a very foolish thing, going into the city today. There could be riots—shooting."

She shrugged. "I didn't know all that was going on. I hadn't listened to the radio."

He stopped his pacing to stand before her. His green eyes scourged her. "Why were you running out on me? We had an agreement."

"I wasn't running out. I was going home for a visit. You read my note."

"You were coming back?"

"Yes."

"I don't believe you."

Now her eyes flashed fire. "I keep my part of an agreement—better than you do!"

"What is that supposed to mean?"

"I seem to recall that you had agreed that our marriage was to be strictly a matter of business, in name only. You broke your word about that on our wedding night."

He flushed darkly. Then he said, "Why were you going home? You are that miserable here?"

"Miserable? Yes."

"You are not treated well? I left orders that you were to have anything you wanted. Miguel would have taken you anywhere in the city. You have money to spend—I set no limits—"

"You don't understand. I was lonely and homesick. I needed to be with my family for a while, near people who love me and care about me. There are some things money can't provide, Jorge Del Toro, although you seem oblivious to that fact!"

"Why didn't you talk with me about this? Why just leave a note and walk out?"

"You were never here. I made the decision this morning. You had other interests to keep you occupied."

Her implication in the phrase "other interests" was lost on him for the moment. He said defensively, "I have explained that to you. These are troubled times for me. The political situation has been in turmoil. I am busy arranging affairs so we can leave this country. The sooner we can get to the States, the sooner you can see your parents. That's what you want, isn't it?"

"Partly."

"Partly?"

"Yes. The main part is that I'll be glad when this marriage is over."

His green eyes glinted darkly. "Is it really so terrible being married to me?"

Terrible? No, she thought, under the right circumstances, it would be heaven. But under these circumstances, it was hell. "Yes," she said, "it is terrible when you deliberately humiliate me."

"How have I done that?"

"By consorting with Consuelo when you are married

to me. Latin women may accept such behavior in their husbands. I find it degrading and humiliating. Our marriage may be nothing but a business arrangement, but I assumed you would show me the respect due a proper wife. You said this marriage was to appear authentic. Couldn't you and she wait the year until our divorce?"

"What makes you think I have been 'consorting' with Consuelo as you put it?"

"Her brother, Rafael, told me. You have been with her several times."

He scowled darkly. "Then you have been with Rafael again!"

Her eyes flashed defiance. "He came here to the house to see me. It was in broad daylight and quite respectable—hardly the clandestine manner in which you and Consuelo have met." Then she blurted out, "Has she become your mistress?" and immediately regretted the question. Her heart had asked before her mind could halt the words.

He scowled more darkly than before, giving her a penetrating look. "Would it really matter to you?"

Inwardly, she thought, *Yes, it matters very much that you care for another woman, and that is why my heart is breaking.* But her stung pride made her eyes glint cold anger, and she said to him, "Sorry to throw a wet blanket on your swollen macho ego, but I couldn't care less, except how it humiliates me, as I said."

Although they were in the same room, they were looking at each other across a mile-wide gulf that separated them.

Finally Del Toro sighed, "We cannot talk without using angry words. We live under the same roof and have shared the same bed. Yet, we are total strangers." Then he said, "Well, whether you like it or not, you are stuck with me here for a little while longer. All transportation in and out of the country has been suspended. It would not be safe for you to venture into the city until the political situation has stabilized."

He stalked out of the room, leaving her to shed more tears of lonely despair. He had not denied that Consuelo was now his mistress. Perhaps she had been all along, with an understanding that she would one day be his wife. That would explain her possessiveness and self-assurance with him. And her determination that JoNell was not going to come between them.

JoNell phoned her mother with the disappointing news that her trip home had been delayed. Then there was nothing to do but wait until the situation changed. She fell into a depression as the days passed, and the airport remained closed. She saw even less of Del Toro than before. He seemed to be making a point of staying away as much as possible, and avoiding her when he was in the house. They had one evening meal together in the dining room, and it was a strained, silent hour.

One night, JoNell was awakened by the fearful trembling that she had come to dread—an earthquake tremor. She stared up at the darkness, her heart pounding furiously. The quivering of her bed stopped and gradually the beat of her heart became normal. Suddenly, her bedroom door opened. Del Toro, in his robe, was silhouetted against the light of the hall. She lay very still, pretending to be asleep, but peering at him through her lashes. He stood in the doorway, looking at her for several minutes, as if to convince himself that the tremor had not awakened or frightened her. At last, he drew back into the hallway, closing her door quietly.

She was no longer frightened, but it was hours before she finally went back to sleep. When she awoke in the morning, she switched on her bedside radio. Listening to the early morning news had become a ritual as she eagerly awaited word of the airport opening. First the announcer talked about seismograph recordings of an earthquake in the mountains, which explained the tremor she had felt last night. Then came news that made her heart bound. The political situation had stabilized. The military was reopening all forms of transportation in and out of the country.

JoNell bounded out of bed. She dressed hurriedly, making plans as she prepared for the trip home. This time she would wait until she had booked a definite flight before phoning her parents. She would call the airport to see about a reservation. Probably the early flights would be crowded. She picked up the telephone.

At that moment, Del Toro burst into the room. She was startled both by his unannounced entrance, and his appearance. He looked haggard, unshaven. His hair was rumpled. Never had she seen him look so disheveled and so distraught.

"You must come with me," he ordered swiftly.

"Where? What are you talking about?"

"There was an earthquake in the mountains last night—"

A sudden icy hand squeezed her heart. "Not the mining village—"

He nodded soberly. "Yes. It looks bad. The seismograph instruments at the university pinpointed the site of the earthquake in that area. I've been trying to contact them, but the telephone lines are down. I finally made contact with one of my mining engineers there who is a ham radio operator. The village has been devastated. A lot of people have been hurt."

"Oh, how awful—" Tears burned JoNell's eyes as memories flashed across her mind of the people who had shown her such friendliness.

Del Toro ran trembling fingers through his dark hair. "JoNell, I need you to fly me there. The bridge into the village was destroyed. We can only get there by air. With the political mess the country is in, there'll be all kinds of red tape and delay before the government does anything. We can't wait for that. I need to get a doctor and medical supplies up there immediately."

He grasped her arm urgently. "I need you, JoNell. If you will do this for me, I will give you what you want more than anything else—your freedom. Gustamente has fled the country; he is no longer a threat to me. You are obviously terribly unhappy married to me. You want to go home. I won't stand in your way or hold you to our bargain any longer. Just help me get aid to those people, and we'll put an end to this marriage."

Chapter 9

JoNell nodded. "Yes, of course I'll help. . . ."

They descended the stairs rapidly. "Miguel will drive you to the airport," Del Toro explained. "That will give you time to get the plane ready. I will join you shortly with a doctor and medical supplies."

The car roared off. JoNell had been so overwhelmed by the unexpected and dramatic events of the last few minutes that she hadn't had time to fully digest the implications. Now she realized how intimately involved Miguel was in what happened at the village. And she suddenly thought of Angelita, that kind, generous woman, who might be lying injured or dead in the rubble of the destroyed village.

Miguel drove in tense silence in marked contrast to his usual humorous chatter. "Are you going to fly to the village with us, Miguel?" JoNell asked gently.

"Not this trip, señora," he replied, the customary joy wrung from his voice. "Señor Del Toro wants to use every bit of space for the doctor and supplies. I will gather more food, bandages, water, that sort of thing. It will take more than one trip to send everything that is needed. Perhaps I can go on the last trip."

"Of course you can. Meanwhile, I'll check on Angelita for you."

"Thank you, señora. I will say prayers and stop by the cathedral and light a candle. . . ."

Miguel deposited her at the airport and sped off. JoNell entered the airport office where she had first met Jorge Del Toro. Memories of their first encounter replayed in her mind. Sadly, she looked around the room, knowing this was to be one of the last times she would ever see the couch where she had sat that fateful day when she had brazenly dared Del Toro to ride with her in the airplane. As badly as she wanted out of the unhappy marriage, she knew that when she left Peru, she would be leaving the only man in the world she would ever truly love. Whenever she looked at another man, the magnificent figure and spirit of Jorge Del Toro would get in the way.

Brushing tears from her eyes, she checked the level of gasoline in the airplane, then drained a small amount through a pet cock to check for moisture condensation in the tanks. After that she rolled the plane out the hangar door. Then she paced back and forth, waiting impatiently. After what seemed like an hour, but was probably no more than thirty minutes, the black Rolls Royce drove up and screeched to a halt. Del Toro jumped out, and with him, a tall, dark man dressed in a black suit. They began carrying boxes from the trunk of the car to the plane. JoNell climbed into the plane and flipped the lever on the rear seat to fold it down in order to make room for the supplies to pass over into the luggage compartment.

That done, JoNell silently joined the two men, carrying some of the lighter boxes herself. Within minutes, they had filled the luggage compartment.

"Can you take off with that much extra weight?" Del Toro asked.

She nodded, hoping that her estimate of the weight of the load was accurate.

They got into the airplane, Del Toro and JoNell in the front, the doctor in the back seat. After they were airborne, Del Toro briefly introduced JoNell to Dr. Torres. Del Toro and the doctor spent the time in the air discussing what additional supplies would be needed and where they could be obtained. They made a list for JoNell to give to Miguel.

JoNell's mind was occupied with worry about landing the plane on the short stretch of meadow that served as a primitive landing strip. The plane was carrying the extra load of medical supplies without complaint, but the added weight would make her landing more hazardous. She was going to have to call on all her reserves of skill to stop the greater momentum of the plane that she knew it would have this time.

When the landing strip came into view, JoNell tuned out the discussion going on between Del Toro and the doctor. She lined the plane up with the grassy strip of land and asked help from a higher source to see her through this landing. She eased the plane down with more skill than she'd realized she possessed. When the wheels touched the turf, she worked the brakes with a controlled fury, her slender fingers squeezing the stick with apprehension.

The plane rolled to a stop with the propeller tickling the tall grass just beyond the clearing. A gasp of relief escaped JoNell's lips, but Del Toro didn't notice. This time, there were no men in the field tending their llamas. There were no happy shouts of "Del Toro! Señor Del Toro!" Only an eerie silence permeated the air. She could already see signs of devastation—huge trees toppled over. And she shivered when she glanced up and saw buzzards circling in the blue sky.

JoNell had seen the aftermath of hurricanes. She

165

knew the devastation a natural disaster could cause. She steeled herself for the grim sights they would see in the village.

Del Toro and the doctor each grabbed a box from the luggage compartment of the plane. JoNell took a smaller one. The three set out on the dusty path that JoNell remembered so well, but thought she'd never see again.

When they reached a point where she remembered seeing the first roofs of dwellings, there was nothing but the blankness of the blue sky. JoNell gasped.

They hurried into the clearing. To the right and left, adobe huts lay in ruins. All that was left standing were a few crumbled adobe walls. A llama rug whipped in the breeze around a scrubby brush. Bits of gaily colored ponchos peeked out from beneath torn sections of straw mats that had once been beds. There wasn't a person stirring in the rubble.

JoNell looked up at Del Toro. His eyes, grim and steely, took in the sight of roofs caved in on shattered dwellings. "Where is everybody?" JoNell asked. She had an eerie sensation of being alone in the world with only Del Toro and Dr. Torres.

"Let's find out," Del Toro said. He led the trio past the section of adobe huts to the part of the village where the brick cottages had stood. Some of them had been completely destroyed. But here and there some houses were intact. Everything looked so different, so chaotic, that JoNell lost her sense of direction. She couldn't determine which had been Angelita's cottage and which had been the cottage she had shared with Del Toro. Then she located their cottage. Only one wall remained standing. Tears burned her eyes. During those brief days she had spent here, that humble cottage had seemed much more like a home than Del Toro's elegant mansion in Lima. And now it was destroyed.

In this area, JoNell saw a few Indian villagers scraping through the rubble of their homes, a blank expression on their faces. One snaggle-toothed old man, his face wrinkled from years in the hot sun, looked at them without seeing. Then a faint light flickered in his fading black eyes. "Señor Del Toro," he called weakly. Then he and Del Toro spoke briefly in the native language.

"The people have all gone to the marketplace," Del Toro explained. "The earthquake did the least damage there."

"Does he know anything about Angelita?" JoNell asked anxiously.

Del Toro spoke to the man again, then shook his head, and motioned them on to the marketplace.

The closer they came to the marketplace, the fewer structures were destroyed. When they rounded the last corner, they came upon a makeshift first-aid station. Injured people were lying on straw mats and llama rugs on the ground. Moans of pain were everywhere. There were anguished sobs of persons bending over some of the deathly still. The children played quietly while cries of pain and sorrow were heard in the background.

Immediately, Del Toro began unpacking medical supplies and the doctor ripped off his coat and went to work over the more seriously hurt. A crowd of men gathered around Del Toro, who rattled to them in their strange dialect. He gestured broadly. They nodded and then were gone.

"They're going to bring the rest of the supplies from the plane," he said. "As soon as it's unloaded, I want you to fly back to Lima for more. Miguel will meet you at the airport."

"But what about Angelita?" JoNell protested. "I can't leave until I know what's happened to her."

Del Toro called to an Indian woman sitting beside a small child on the ground. She mumbled something incomprehensible to JoNell. Del Toro motioned for JoNell to follow her. She led the way to the interior of the market building. There, they found more injured. Anxiously, JoNell searched among the dark-haired women. Finally, she spied a familiar head. Immense relief flooded her. She made her way through the rows of injured and to the side of Angelita.

The woman was crooning softly to a man JoNell recognized as Angelita's escort the night of the special festival.

"Angelita! I'm so glad you're all right."

The woman turned to look at her. Her face was deeply lined with grief and fatigue. Her eyes widened with surprise. "JoNell! What are you doing here?"

"I came to help," she said simply. "Is this your friend, Carlos?"

"Yes," Angelita said tearfully. "He has been badly injured, and he is in such pain. If only we had a doctor."

"You do now," JoNell reassured her. "Jorge had me fly a doctor here with medical supplies. He's outside the marketplace right now, taking care of the injured."

"Oh, *gracias por Dios,*" she wept. "We knew Jorge would come to help us. Please tell the doctor to hurry."

"I will," JoNell promised. She rejoined Del Toro and they went to tell Dr. Torres about the injured Carlos.

"I'll walk back to the plane with you," Del Toro said. "But you'll have to fly back by yourself. They need me to help here."

"Yes, I know." She felt a sudden wave of pride to be walking beside this big man. In his commanding way, he was a tower of strength here in the mining village. Miguel had spoken the truth when he said the people here loved and respected him. She remembered how Angelita had said with simple faith, "We knew Jorge would come to help us."

They were halfway to the airplane when they heard a terrified shriek. They both responded immediately, running in the direction of the agonized cry. Del Toro outdistanced JoNell considerably. Her breathing was labored from the thin oxygen. She arrived in front of a crumbling hut to find a young woman sobbing hysterically and pointing to the rubble.

Del Toro shoved the woman aside roughly. "Keep her here," he ordered. "No matter what, don't let her follow me."

JoNell gasped when she saw what was causing the woman's agitation. Sticking out from under the crumbled adobe was a tiny arm clutching a toy llama. Poised right above the debris was a huge slab of heavy adobe hanging precariously on more wreckage. Del Toro maneuvered gingerly through the mangled bits of furniture and caved in roof. JoNell's mouth went dry. She clutched the woman's shoulders with a fierceness born of panic. At any moment, the slab could tumble free from its tenuous support and come crashing down on Del Toro and the child, burying them both in a rock-like grave. Del Toro bent over the little arm and began gently lifting pieces of plaster and wreckage. A gust of wind blew through the ruined building and the adobe slab swayed menacingly over Del Toro's head. He paused, looked up momentarily, then resumed this task with the same gentleness, but at a faster pace. The young woman began to babble hysterically again. She fought to pull free of JoNell's clutch.

"I'm not sure I can hold her," JoNell yelled in fright.

"Slap her hard across the face," Del Toro commanded.

"What?" she asked incredulously.

"Do what I say!"

JoNell obeyed, swinging her palm as hard as she could.

The young woman gasped. But the glassy look faded from her eyes. She collapsed into JoNell's arms, sobbing, but no longer struggling to free herself.

JoNell held the woman and turned her attention back to Del Toro. He had uncovered the upper half of a small, dark boy with curly black hair. Again the wreckage groaned, and the adobe wall teetered precariously.

"Hurry!" JoNell called frantically. "It's not going to hang there much longer."

Del Toro now began to dig furiously at the rubble. He pulled on the boy's torso, but still could not free him. He dug still further until he uncovered a bed frame which was pinning the boy's small foot. Perspiration glistened on his forehead. His powerful muscles bulged as he lifted the bed frame which was weighed down with piles of rubble. At last he was able to free the limp child. The young woman in JoNell's arms began sobbing again.

There was a loud *crunch!* JoNell screamed. The adobe slab that had been threatening the lives of Del Toro and the boy came crashing down, missing them by inches as he darted out of the way.

JoNell's knees threatened to give way. The young woman rushed to Del Toro and the boy. She was again babbling tearfully.

Del Toro interpreted for JoNell. "She has been searching for the boy ever since the earthquake. She found him just as we were passing by. The boy is still breathing. We're going to take him to Dr. Torres. You go on back to Lima for more supplies."

JoNell nodded, wiping her damp palms on her jump suit. Del Toro was dusty and sweat-stained. His shirt had been torn, revealing powerful muscles. He was magnificent. JoNell remembered the day on the polo grounds when she had likened him to a fierce conquistador. Her throat felt tight as admiration and love for him welled up in her.

She turned quickly, before he saw what was in her eyes. She hurried away, down the dusty lane, half blinded by tears. After this crisis was over, there would be a quick divorce. She would return to the States and probably never see Jorge Del Toro again. But the memory of his strength and bravery would remain a part of her for as long as she lived.

JoNell made her second round trip with supplies from Lima safely. As the men unloaded the plane, she marveled at the calm manner in which Del Toro had taken charge of the village. He had organized the men into clean-up crews and had set up a portable kitchen. The high altitude and thin oxygen did not seem to affect him. His energy seemed boundless. Where the village had appeared stunned and demoralized when JoNell first surveyed the wreckage, now there was a spirit of hope and optimism. And she knew the whole village was drawing its strength from Jorge Del Toro.

JoNell flew back to Lima for her final load of supplies with a feeling of deep sadness. She truly felt sorry for herself that her marriage to this remarkable man had not been a real marriage. How empty her life was going to be. . . .

This time Miguel was her passenger on the flight back to the village. JoNell took off with a feeling of apprehension. This final load was heavier than the others. But so much was needed that she and Miguel had crammed every inch of space with supplies. Miguel added to the weight problem. He was not a light man. He weighed in excess of two hundred pounds, she was sure. But darkness was fast approaching, and the villagers were in dire need of every ounce of supplies she could ferry in. So she took a chance that the plane could bear the load.

After a sluggish takeoff, JoNell concentrated on trying to maintain the right altitude. She and Miguel spoke little, each too wrapped up in concern over the village to engage in idle chatter. Approaching nightfall added to JoNell's worries. Was she cutting the time estimate too thin? With the added weight and no tail wind, the flight was taking much longer than she had planned. Already the jungle below was a mass of twilight shadows. Sunset among the mountain peaks was a magnificent sight, with golden rays arcing across the violet sky. Another time she would have felt a breathless thrill at the sight. But now all she could think of was how to make a landing on that skimpy meadow in the dark. Knowing how resourceful Del Toro was, she thought he'd no doubt have the men build bonfires along the landing strip. But would that be enough?

She was debating whether the prudent thing to do would be to go back to Lima and start out in the morning when the plane suddenly began to sputter. Her gaze darted to the gas tank gauge. There was plenty of fuel. The problem was something else. She worked the throttle back and forth to try and restore power. She breathed easier when the engine coughed back to life and purred contentedly. But her relief was short-lived. Again the engine began missing. JoNell's gaze raced over the instruments. Her eyes widened when she saw the temperature gauge. It was inching into the danger zone. Her mouth felt dry. She pulled all the tricks she could think of out of her mental bag of airplane skills, but nothing helped. The altimeter needle began to swing downward. The engine ran rougher and rougher.

"What's the matter?" Miguel asked nervously.

"I'm not sure," JoNell admitted, "but all that weight in the back of the plane isn't helping matters any."

"Can we make it to the village?"

"I don't know, Miguel," she confessed, her hands growing clammy. "We're going down fast. We may have to make a forced landing."

"You mean we're going to crash?" Miguel asked fearfully.

"No," she tried to reassure him, "I'll just have to find a place to land here. If I can find a smooth, flat surface, I can land the plane just like at an airport."

"But then what do we do? We are many miles from civilization here in the mountains."

"I'll radio for help. I'll give our position as near as I can figure it. Then we may have to wait until a search party finds us. It may take a while, but we have a whole plane full of supplies. We won't starve, at least—"

The engine suddenly died completely. There was an eerie silence broken only by the lonely moan of the wind around the airplane.

"*Madre de Dios,*" Miguel whimpered. He clasped his hands and began to pray.

JoNell hoped Miguel had a good patron saint because they were going to need the help of providence. She saw only occasional smooth patches in the rocky terrain that was fast zooming up toward them.

Quickly, she had to make her decision. She selected a spot that appeared to be somewhat smoother, although there wasn't much from which to choose. Her hands gripped the stick tensely. She had practiced forced landings many times. But never had she been confronted with such poor choices for a landing site. In spite of her confidence in her flying ability, she knew this was a situation that would put all her skills to the utmost test.

Suddenly, the ground came up fast. JoNell pulled back on the stick, trying to keep the plane from nosing over. She had to put down in a small clearing surrounded by trees on three sides with a sheer drop into a

173

canyon on the fourth side. The plane rolled briskly toward the edge of the cliff, threatening to shoot off into empty space. JoNell mashed the foot pedals to the right to avoid rolling over the cliff. The plane did a ground loop. There was a rending, shuddering crash as they struck a boulder.

JoNell sat stunned in the pilot's seat. Somewhere a bird squawked. She became conscious of pain inching up her left leg. She looked at Miguel, whose head was slumped forward, his chin touching his chest.

"Miguel?" she asked painfully.

He did not answer.

Chapter 10

JoNell reached quickly for his wrist. Her fingers searched for a pulse, couldn't find one, then at last did. The pulse was weak, but steady. She drew a shuddering gasp of relief.

The pain in her leg was growing more intense. She pulled her jump suit pant leg up and saw a long, ragged gash in the calf of her leg. It was bleeding profusely.

She looked around the wreckage of the cabin. Then she remembered the radio and tried it. She heard nothing but static. The receiver was not working. Could she transmit? She tried, sending out "Mayday" calls in Spanish, giving her location as well as she could reckon it. But she had no way of knowing if the transmitter was working. She had the dismal feeling that she was wasting her breath.

JoNell unbuckled her seat belt and tried lifting her body from the confines of the airplane's interior which had been smashed in around them. When she was able to free herself, she unbuckled Miguel's seat belt, but his considerable weight proved impossible for her to move.

His breathing was shallow. He remained unconscious. His color was not good. JoNell was frightened for him.

She thought that she must try to find help. Miguel needed medical attention. They couldn't wait for hours, maybe days, for searching parties to find them.

JoNell climbed down from the plane. The right wing was flattened back over the cockpit. The front of the plane was crumpled like a ball of wastepaper. She winced at the sight of the wreckage.

When her right foot touched the ground, searing pain shot up her leg, making her cry out. She crumpled to the ground. The leg was hurt worse than she'd first thought. There must be some torn ligaments in addition to the deep cut. The leg couldn't support her weight.

She lay on the ground, gathering her strength. Then she dragged herself back into the plane. By now the sun had disappeared behind the mountain peaks. The long shadows had turned into twilight. Soon they would be swallowed by inky darkness.

She rummaged around in the wreckage that littered the cabin until she found a flashlight. She was going to need that light in the dark hours ahead. Next, she painfully shoved and pushed the boxes around until she located one containing medical supplies. With a pair of scissors she found in the box, she cut away the leg of her jump suit. Then she made a bandage out of a roll of gauze and tied it tightly around the gash that was bleeding steadily. In no time, the bandage was soaked red. She replaced it with a fresh wrapping. She was near the ragged edge of panic. What if she couldn't stop the bleeding? There was no telling how much blood she had already lost. Red stains were splattered all over the cabin. Waves of dizziness assaulted her, either from the loss of blood or shock and pain.

She rummaged through the box of supplies. It contained numerous bottles of drugs. She tried to read the labels by the light of her flash, but they were all generic names in Spanish. She had no idea what they were. But she did find a box of American brand aspirin, and she quickly swallowed two tablets.

Her leg did not stop bleeding until she had applied the third tight bandage. With that under control, she worked her way back around to where Miguel still sat slumped over, unconscious. Again she felt for his pulse. It was the same as before, a weak thread. JoNell now became aware of an ugly bruise on the side of his head that was becoming swollen. He'd evidently suffered a severe head injury. He might have a concussion or worse, a fractured skull with internal, cerebral bleeding.

A wave of desperation seized her, and with it an overpowering sense of guilt. She should never have tried to take off with the plane so heavily overloaded this close to nightfall. If Miguel lost his life, she'd have her poor judgment to blame.

She tried the radio again, giving her location and sending an urgent call for help. "Please. . . ." she begged, tears streaming down her cheeks. "We need help. Please hurry and find us. . . ."

But she still did not know if the transmitter was working. She could hear nothing on the receiver part of the radio.

Then she became aware of a new threat that turned her blood to ice—the unmistakable smell of gasoline. The crash must have ruptured a fuel line or a tank. If there were the slightest spark, they would die a fiery death in the plane.

Again, she tried her best to move Miguel. She tugged and lifted with what strength she had left. But after a bit she fell back in her seat, panting and damp with perspiration. There was no way she could move him. The door on his side was jammed solidly shut. And she did not have the strength to lift the heavy man across her seat and out of the door on her side of the cabin.

She began to shiver. With darkness came the bone penetrating chill of the night air at high altitude. On this trip, their cargo was only boxes of medical supplies. No blankets. Nothing to wrap up with against the cold.

She shone her flashlight over the boxes of supplies in the vain hope that she could find something that could help them. The light touched several pairs of crutches. When she saw them, a plan born of desperation began forming in her mind.

She located her map and studied it carefully in the glow of her flashlight. They were closer to the mining village than she had first thought. Actually, they had gotten to within about fifteen kilometers of their destination when they went down. Translated into miles, they were roughly ten miles from the village.

But ten miles could as well be a thousand if nobody knew they were here. They could easily sit here a week or longer as searching parties combed this wild, mountainous terrain, looking for them. That would be all right if neither of them had been injured. They had food and water to sustain them. But Miguel urgently needed medical attention.

As she was pondering the situation, she heard the distant rumble of thunder. She looked anxiously out of the open door on her side and saw lightning flashes along the eastern horizon. A worried frown crossed her brow. An electrical storm in the mountains could be an ominous threat to them. If a bolt of lightning struck around this gasoline soaked wreckage. . . .

She shuddered.

The approaching storm removed any remaining indecision she had. Now she knew she had to find help to get Miguel out of the plane and to a doctor. And she had to do it soon.

Moving quickly before she lost her nerve, she tossed the crutches out, and then scrambled down after them. The aspirin had eased the pain of her leg a bit. With a pair of crutches to help, she found she was able to navigate. It was slow and painful going over the rough terrain, but she thought with luck she might be able to reach the village by morning. That is, if she didn't get lost, or didn't get bitten by a snake in the underbrush, or if she didn't freeze to death.

The cold air searched relentlessly through her flimsy jump suit and chilled her to the bone. How careless of her not to have brought a jacket! All she'd had on her mind today was the desperate plight of the village people.

She knew she must travel due west. She remembered the spot where the sun had gone down between two mountain peaks, and set her course in that direction. With some experimentation, she found she was able to discard one of the crutches and get along with just the left crutch to help take the weight off her injured leg. That left her right hand free to hold the flashlight. Its flashing beam was a slender shaft of light that enabled her to find the best path over the rough ground.

Once she left the clearing where the plane had crashed she found herself in inky blackness under a mass of trees. She was surrounded by a tangled growth of vines and underbrush. As she struggled along, she heard the strange night sounds of the jungle around her. Invisible wings would suddenly flutter above her. Something rustled in the underbrush near her ankle. She tried not to think about the kinds of wild beasts that lurked in this primitive area—pythons that could crush a human to death in minutes, panthers that could spring from a tree on their prey, poisonous reptiles slithering through the underbrush. . . .

She had been making her painful, limping progress for about an hour when the storm struck. The thunder had been growing louder, the lightning steadily more brilliant. And suddenly, great torrents of rain slashed down.

She was soaked to the skin within minutes. Her teeth were chattering. She began whimpering with fright.

Great searing flashes of lightning were exploding all around. There were crackling reports like cannons going off as bolts of lightning ripped into giant trees, splitting them apart and sending branches crashing down.

She thought about poor Miguel, trapped in the gasoline soaked airplane with lightning striking all around, and she sobbed with despair and terror.

The ground was becoming a soggy, slippery quagmire. Wet leaves and branches slapped at her. She fell down, struggled to her feet, slipped and fell down again. Somehow she got up, but a few feet further on, she fell hard. The flashlight was knocked from her hand and went tumbling down a ravine. She heard a tinkle of glass as it smashed against a rock far below. Now there was only inky blackness split apart by the blue-white flashes of lightning.

JoNell huddled on the ground, sobbing frantically. As long as she'd had the flashlight, she had clung to a slender thread of hope. The flashlight had been like a friend, a companion. It had been her one weapon against the terrifying blackness of the jungle night. And she'd tried to believe that its flashing light frightened off predatory animals.

But now she was totally at the mercy of the savage night, half frozen, and helplessly lost. She knew she was going to die here, terrified and utterly alone.

Somehow she struggled to her feet. Now she was driven by sheer panic, the instinct to flee from danger. She pushed her way through the underbrush, ignoring the throbbing pain in her leg. She no longer had any sense of direction. There was only the primitive need to run.

Then the ground gave way. She pitched headlong into empty space. A scream was on her lips, but was never uttered. She was swallowed by blackness, a void into which she sank endlessly down, down, down into oblivion. . . .

Consciousness was at first only fragmentary. There was white all around her. Faces peering down at her. A woman with a nurse's cap. A white ceiling. Darkness again.

Another fragment. A man's quiet voice. White again. He wore a white jacket. She saw a hypodermic needle in his hand poised over her arm. She looked away. Another face. Jorge Del Toro. Very pale, very worried. She licked her dry lips. She wanted to say something to him. But the needle pricked her arm. And then she felt very comfortable and sleepy.

She awoke and it was hard to breathe. Her chest hurt. She tried to complain. She looked around and saw only a plastic tent. She was trapped under the clear plastic tent. With a cry, she tried to sit up. But firm hands pushed her back. The reassuring voices again. The prick of the needle. Again the curtain of drowsiness closing around her.

The next time, her surroundings were in sharper focus. The plastic tent was gone. She could breathe more easily. The woman with the nurse's cap looked down at her and smiled. "Well, we're much better today, aren't we?"

She was talking Spanish. Why was she talking Spanish? Cuban, perhaps. So many in south Florida, now.

JoNell swallowed and tried her voice. "Is my mother here?" she asked in English.

The pretty nurse smiled, her eyes uncomprehending. "Would you be so kind as to speak in Spanish, señora? I regret that my English is very poor. Your husband told us you are quite fluent in our language."

"My husband?" JoNell asked blankly in Spanish.

180

"Yes. He has hardly left your bedside for the past week. He just stepped out now for a bite to eat, but he will be back soon. He will be so happy that you are awake." She smiled and rolled her eyes. "Such a handsome man. You are a lucky señora."

"My husband—" JoNell repeated. She was very confused. She looked around the room. "Where is this place?"

"You are in the hospital in Lima, señora."

"Lima?" JoNell was growing more confused.

"Yes, you have been very ill, but you are much better now."

"I'm afraid I'm kind of mixed up. How did I get here?"

The nurse was busy fluffing her pillow. "You have a delightful accent, señora. It's *Cubano,* is it not? I once had a cousin from Cuba who visited us. She spoke with the kind of lisp you use."

JoNell closed her eyes. Evidently the nurse was not going to give her any information. Her mind was dulled and sluggish from medication. She felt as if she were groping in a fog for that elusive part of her mind that stored memories.

But she was too tired to make the effort. She dozed for a while. Then she sighed and opened her eyes, feeling rested. She looked into the face of the most incredibly handsome man she had ever seen. For a fraction of a second he was a stranger to her. Then he was Jorge Del Toro, her husband.

"Jorge!" she whispered.

He was smiling, but his green eyes were filled with tears. She had never seen tears in his eyes before. She felt his big powerful hand close over hers. "Sh," he murmured softly. "You are all right now, JoNell. Everything is all right. But you must rest, the doctor said."

"But what am I doing here?"

And then, all in a rush, she remembered.

Everything. . . .

She struggled to sit up, her eyes wide with terror. "Miguel! He's trapped in the plane. He's badly hurt. Jorge—you must get him out—"

Gently, but firmly, he pushed her back. "JoNell, Miguel is safe. We got him out of the plane. He's fine. He left the hospital yesterday."

"Yesterday?" she stammered. "But we crashed yesterday—"

"No," he said quietly. "You crashed a week ago, JoNell."

She stared at him incredulously. "A week ago! But—but where have I been?"

"Right here, most of the time, although I'm afraid for a little while you were very close to the angels."

"But how did I get here? The last thing I remember—" She frowned, straining to push away the last of the fog. "Yes, I remember. There was a storm. I was falling. . . ."

"You fell into a deep ravine. We found you there about dawn the next morning. Actually, you were less than a kilometer from the plane. You'd walked in a circle."

"But in that awful wilderness. How did you ever find us?"

"When you didn't return with the last load of supplies, we became worried. We used the ham short-wave radio in the village to contact the airport in Lima. They said they had received a faint radio signal from you that you were down in the mountains, and gave your approximate location."

"Then my radio was working!"

"Yes. They were planning to send a helicopter from Lima to search for you as soon as it was light. But we didn't want to wait that long. From the location they gave, I knew you were not more than fifteen or twenty kilometers from the village. A storm was coming up. I had no intention of leaving you out there in the jungle all night. Some of my Indian friends in the village know that region as well as most people know the way to the bathrooms in their homes. We started out immediately to find you. We located the plane about midnight and got Miguel out. It wasn't that easy to find you. We searched the area the rest of the night. The sun was coming up when one of my men located your trail. There were broken branches, some drops of blood on weeds that had brushed against your leg. We found the flashlight. And, at last we found you. We carried you to the village where Dr. Torres administered first aid. Then the helicopter from Lima arrived, and we flew you and Miguel here to the hospital. Actually, Miguel got off lighter than you did. He had a pretty bad concussion, but recovered quickly. You, on the other hand, were suffering from shock and exposure which went into pneumonia. But now all that is over. You only have to rest and recuperate."

JoNell remembered what the nurse had said, that Del Toro had scarcely left her bedside for the past week. She could see deep lines of fatigue and worry etched in his face. He seemed older. She wondered curiously why he had been so concerned about her. Then she realized that he must have felt responsible for her accident and close brush with death. After all, it was he who had asked her to ferry the supplies to the village. If he had not put her in that position, she would have been safely on her way home to Florida.

The nurse came in with a small glass of bitter tasting medicine. JoNell swallowed it, then wanted to ask a lot more questions. But suddenly she became very sleepy. Her tongue was heavy. She thought, "Darn it, that medicine was a sedative. . . ." and then she slept again.

The next time she awoke, Del Toro was gone. She assumed that she was out of danger now, and he no longer felt obligated to keep a vigil by her bed.

She slept again, and the next morning felt strong enough to sit up. She had her first solid food for breakfast. Then the nurse helped comb her hair and apply some light makeup. She felt almost human again.

Becoming more aware of her surroundings now, she realized with a twinge of disappointment that there were no flowers in the room. "You'd think, after the way he had bushels of roses carted into my room at the mansion, Del Toro could have sent a few up here," she thought, then laughed at herself. There was no reason for him to send flowers here. The only reason he had deluged her with roses at first was when he was giving her the old Latin flattery bit. The time for such romantic foolishness ended when their relationship became nothing but a business agreement.

Just the same, she wished he'd had a few delivered to her room.

The phone in her room rang. The nurse answered it, then brought it to the bed. "It is your mother, calling from North America. She has phoned every day to talk with your husband. He has kept her informed about your progress."

JoNell and her mother had a tearful reunion by long distance. Her father was on the extension, so she talked with him, too, and with her Uncle Edgar. Her mother had wanted to fly to Lima, but didn't think it wise to leave her father alone. And Del Toro had assured them that JoNell was getting the best medical care money could buy.

JoNell realized from the things her mother said, that Del Toro had kept from the family how seriously ill she had actually been, not wanting to alarm them. They assumed she had a respiratory illness, but had never been in any actual danger. JoNell was grateful to Del Toro for that. There had been no use in alarming her mother and father, especially considering her father's heart condition.

She spent the rest of the morning dozing and watching a television program. After lunch, a nurse came in to arrange her pillows and smooth her bed. "Do you feel up to having a visitor? Your husband is outside."

JoNell felt her heart suddenly beating faster. "Yes," she said quickly. Then reminded herself that this would probably be one of the last times she would see Del Toro.

"Good afternoon," he said solemnly. "How are you feeling?"

"Much better, thank you."

He was holding a single long-stemmed red rose.

"Is that rose for me?"

"Yes."

"It's beautiful."

He placed the rose in a small white vase beside her bed. He stood looking at it thoughtfully, turning the stem in his fingers.

"How is the village?"

"It's slowly recovering."

"And Angelita and her Carlos?"

"Angelita is fine. Carlos had some broken bones. We've brought him to Lima for treatment, but he'll be all right."

"And the little boy you pulled out of the wreckage of the house?"

"He, too, we brought to Lima for special treatment. The doctors tell us he will recover, but it's going to take several operations before he can walk again."

"And you'll pay for the treatment, won't you? I can see why the village depends on you so."

185

He didn't answer. He was still looking at the rose. Then he said quietly, "JoNell, I am setting you free, as I promised. I am arranging the divorce so it will go quickly and quietly. In such matters it sometimes helps to have some influence and political pull. It won't be necessary for you to appear in court. As soon as you are able to travel, I'll arrange first-class passage on a jetliner. You have fulfilled your obligation to me."

JoNell tried hard to hold back her tears. She managed to keep her voice from breaking, and said evenly, "That's fine."

There was silence.

Then she said, "Will you be all right now? I mean the political thing?"

"Oh, yes. Gustamente has fled the country. I'm all right."

"So you don't need an American wife any longer."

A crooked, sad smile touched his handsome features. "I never did need an American wife. Not for that reason."

She looked at him blankly. "What?"

He sighed. "I must now confess, JoNell. I have not been totally honest with you. No, I should say I haven't been honest at all."

A stinging flush rose to her cheeks. "You don't have to make any confessions about Consuelo. I—"

He waved his hand impatiently. "Please forget about Consuelo. She means nothing to me."

JoNell's jaw dropped. "What? But—but—"

"I don't want to talk about Consuelo. I want to talk about the reason I asked you to marry me. The truth is, I lied to you about needing an American wife to get me into the United States in a hurry. You see, my parents were in the United States on business when I was born. My mother was a citizen of your country. Since I was born there, I too, am a citizen of the United States.

When we were back in this country, it was an easy matter for rich business people to get a Peruvian doctor to make out a Peruvian birth certificate for me, for citizenship purposes in this country. But by birth, I am not Peruvian. I am as much an American as you, if I wish to claim United States citizenship."

JoNell was speechless. Finally, she shook her head in bewilderment. "Then why did you trick me into marrying you?"

He fell silent. He sat in a chair near the bed and looked down at his large, strong fingers spread out on his knees. "I couldn't think of any other way of keeping you here close to me."

She stared at him.

He made a gesture with his hand. "Forgive me, JoNell. I know you are going to hate me even more than you already do. But I can't send you back to the United States without telling you the truth. You remember you had made up your mind to despise me. The minute we finished the flying lessons, you packed to leave. You couldn't get out of my house fast enough. I had to think fast, and on the spur of the moment, came up with the idea of the 'business arrangement' wedding. It was—" he said humbly, "a desperate measure of a man hopelessly in love with a woman who hated him."

JoNell felt dazed. She tried to grasp the full import of what he was telling her. She was too much in a state of shock to fully comprehend the meaning.

"It was insane, I know," he admitted. "I had the crazy notion that if you lived with me for a while as my wife, got used to my kind of life and the things I could give you, perhaps you would grow to love me. But—" he shook his head sadly. "You only hated me more."

JoNell finally managed to speak. "But—you never said—you never told me—" she whispered.

"Oh, yes, but I did. In many ways, right from the start. The first lesson. That day we first kissed on the beach. The notes I sent with the flowers. You did not believe me. You were insulted. You said I was just handing you the customary line of Latin flattery. And it is true, Latin men do like to flatter their women in that manner. But I was sincere. However, since that approach seemed only to offend you, I decided to 'play it cool' as you say in America. I would simply be myself. I would let you see me as I am, the good sides and the bad for what they are worth. I would let you judge me as a man. There were moments—when we shared passion—that I was filled with hope. But afterward, you were always angry with yourself for responding to me, angry with me for awakening that response. You said it was only a physical thing, and that it did not reach your heart."

Because I was afraid, she thought. *Afraid to admit how I did feel, not wanting to be hurt. Hate was my only weapon.*

JoNell was clutching icy hands under the sheets, trying not to let him see how her fingers were trembling. Could he see the way her heart was pounding? She thought surely he must be able to hear it.

She whispered unsteadily, "But Consuelo Garcia, you didn't deny that you were seeing her."

"Oh, Consuelo, that little spoiled brat!" he exclaimed impatiently. "Yes, I had a cocktail with her at the country club one afternoon. And I met her for dinner one evening. She wanted to talk to me about her family's finances. She's a mercenary little thing. She's always had her cap set for me because of my money. I never felt that way about her. I agreed to loan her family some money. After all, her father and my father were best friends. I felt I owed it to them. But you seemed so angry—jealous, I hoped. I let you think

I'd had a romantic meeting with her, wishing to use the old weapon of jealousy. But that didn't work, either."

Del Toro arose. Gravely, he took the exquisite, long-stemmed rose from the vase and placed it on the pillow beside her. "JoNell, I sent you all those dozens of roses when you first came as a symbol of how much I loved you, but you never responded. Now I give you this one red rose as a symbol of my heart which you will take with you wherever you go."

Tears had half blinded her. "It sounds so pretty when you say it that way in Spanish," she choked. "Do you really mean it? I am free to go as soon as I am well?"

He nodded, his eyes sad. "Yes. Whenever you wish."

She let the tears trickle down her cheeks. "But what if I don't want to go?" she asked.

His green eyes looked startled. "What do you mean?"

"I mean that I like it when you say those pretty things to me in Spanish. I like it when you send me flowers, and when you are strong the way you were in the village, and when you are tender the way you are now. I've never, ever known a man like you, Jorge Del Toro. I'm not sure when I fell in love with you. Maybe the first time you walked into that airport office, looking like you owned the whole darn airfield. Or when you kissed me on the beach. Or on our wedding night. I know when I *realized* I was in love with you. It was when we were in the mountain village that first time. Didn't you know I realized I was in love with you then, Jorge?"

As she talked, his green eyes had gone from dark amber to flashing jade. His face had brightened with unbelieving happiness. "JoNell—JoNell—do you really mean it!" he cried.

She nodded, too choked up to say more.

He sat on the edge of the bed, gathering her up in his arms. "My beloved . . . my heart. . . ." he said, raining kisses on her face and throat.

"Easy," she laughed unsteadily. "I'm not *that* well yet."

"But you will be soon. JoNell, are you sure? Did I hear you right? You do love me?"

"Yes, my darling," she laughed. "Very, very much."

He kissed her again. She could feel him trembling with joy and excitement. "We'll have a honeymoon you'll remember a lifetime. Maybe we'll go around the world!"

"How about to Florida?"

"Whatever you want." He shook his head in bewilderment. "You always seemed so angry with me. We could never talk without having angry words. In the village, I gave you that necklace because I loved you, but you threw it back in my face with anger."

"Only because I thought it was a kind of payment for acting like your wife. I was angry because I thought you were going to wind up breaking my heart, and I hated you for that. It was the one thing I'd promised myself I wouldn't let happen."

The nurse came into the room, interrupting them. Del Toro quickly got up from the bed, looking flushed.

"Time for your medicine," the pretty young nurse said, giving JoNell a pill. She shot Del Toro a flirtatious glance and swung her hips walking out of the room.

"I guess I'm going to have to get used to that, having the most handsome husband in the world," JoNell grinned.

"What?"

She realized with a happy glow that Jorge had been totally oblivious to the nurse.

Huskily, she whispered, "Come here, my conquistador. I'm feeling stronger by the minute."

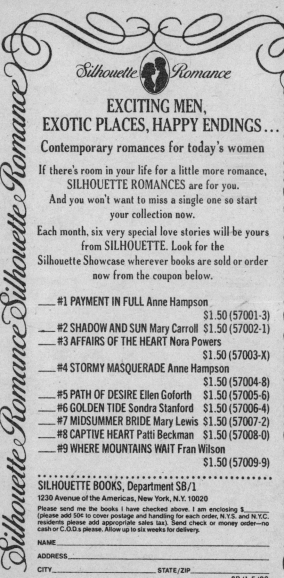